CW01500532

It Worked Fifteen Minutes Ago
Copyright © 2025 by B.A. Ritzenthaler
All rights reserved.

This is a work of fiction. Names, characters, places, and incidents are either products of the author's imagination or used fictitiously. Any resemblance to actual events, locales, or persons, living or dead, is entirely coincidental... unless you were there. In which case, you know who you are.

Cover and Interior Design: B.A. Ritzenthaler
ISBN: 9798296549235
First Edition
Printed in the United States of America
Published by Ritzenthaler Publishing
baritzenthaler.author@gmail.com

To Susan:
For twenty years of putting up with my sea stories,
dad jokes, and midnight typing marathons
—this one's for you.

For those who serve unselfishly
you are the best of us.

And for Hudson
my grandson and, conveniently,
the name of the ship that carried this story.

"Every sea story floats somewhere above the locker. Just don't ask how deep the truth goes."
Found scrawled on a bulkhead

# Table of Contents

# Foreword

The sea story is as old as men sailing on reed canoes and as common as a fisherman lying about the size of his bass.

Every sea story contains a dose of truth. Just enough to keep it entertaining.

Here's the truth about this fictional sea ditty: the characters are an amalgamation of several people rolled into one, unless they're not. The names have all been made up to protect the innocent.

The stories happened exactly as I'm telling you.

Or somewhat like I'm telling you.

Or maybe not at all.

There's always some truth in a sea story. The lesson, if there is one, usually gets delivered in a far more entertaining way than a 150-slide PowerPoint.

So sit back, relax, and enjoy the ride.

There might be a lesson here if you're paying attention.

Or maybe it's just a bunch of bullshit to pass the time.

You'll never know unless you were there.

Either way—I hope you enjoy it.

# Prologue

It's easy to romanticize life at sea when you're watching a sunset from the weather deck, the wind just right, the ocean behaving. In those moments, even the old-timers stop and stare. There's a hush that falls over everyone, even the chaos junkies. The ship steadies itself. The horizon calms you. Your heartbeat slows. Everything just feels... right.

But that's not the story I'm telling.

I'm telling you about everything else; the parts where the machinery fails, the people snap, the medical calls don't go by the book, and command decisions make you question your own sanity. I'm telling you about a world held together with zip ties, duct tape, and hope.

I spent decades on Navy ships and Military Sealift Command vessels. I was the Independent Duty Corpsman and Medical Services Officer, the only medical provider onboard. No backup. No doctor down the hall. Just me, a med bag, and whatever I could MacGyver out of an inventory that hadn't been updated since Desert Storm.

You learn fast in that environment, or you leave. You learn when to follow protocol and when to throw the book overboard. You learn how to deliver a baby, treat a heart attack, pull a guy out of a suicidal spiral, and sew up a drunken engineer's forehead, all in the same week. And you do it with a straight face, because someone has to.

This isn't a story about heroism. It's about endurance. It's about laughing when everything's broken. It's about the quiet moments after midnight when the whole ship creaks and groans like it's telling you secrets. It's about the absurdity, the exhaustion, and the unexpected grace that show up in the middle of nowhere.

My name is Jack Davidson, and I've been out there longer than I ever intended.

It's about a life that worked:
fifteen minutes ago.

# Chapter 1—The HUDSON

If you're the kind of cheater who flips to the last page to see if a book is worth reading, don't bother. I'll save you the trouble: I walk off the ship. In protest, no less.

But that's not the story. The story is everything that happened in between; glorious, idiotic, a little sad, and absolutely unforgettable.

A quick disclaimer before we get rolling. The Military Sealift Command is like any other outfit that sails. It's a job at sea. And the sea? It doesn't give a damn who you are. Salt eats everything; gear, metal, people.

Day and night.

The only reason ships don't sink to the bottom is that men and women fight like hell every day to keep them floating.

This all happened on the HUDSON, but it could have been any ship, anywhere.

\* \* \*

Orders from Norfolk put me on a flight halfway around the world. I won't bore you with all the details, unless someone buys me a drink and asks. Bottom line, I flew from San Diego to L.A., to Tokyo, to Singapore. Then, after two weeks of bureaucratic purgatory in Singapore, I finally landed in Diego Garcia.

Never heard of it? Not surprised. In U.S. and British military circles, it's called "the footprint of freedom."

To the rest of the world, it doesn't exist.

Just a spit of land seven degrees south of the equator, floating in the middle of the Indian Ocean. Home to an airfield, a harbor, and a bunch of stuff the Air Force and Navy don't want to talk about.

But none of that matters. What matters is this: this is where the story begins, where I first stepped aboard the USNS Hudson.

A little about the HUDSON. The USNS Hudson (T-AO 250) is an auxiliary oiler owned by the U.S. Navy and manned by Merchant Mariners, civilians employed by the Navy known as CIVMARs. Many are Navy vets. Some, like me, are retired sailors who apparently didn't get enough sea time the first go-round.

It's named after the Hudson River, like its sister ships are named after rivers, Kanawha, Pecos, Big Horn, Tippecanoe, Guadalupe, Patuxent, Yukon, Laramie, and the Rock.

\* \* \*

I expected the heat to slap me. Instead, a breeze rolled across the island and made it bearable. We stepped off the plane onto the tarmac and into a terminal no bigger than a small-town post office. After the obligatory customs check, I walked into the "Arrivals" area and scanned the faces.

That's when I saw her, a tall blonde in tired clothes and steel-toed boots, holding a yellow notepad with my name and title scribbled in Sharpie:

MSO John Davidson.

I walked over to her and extended a hand, "Hi, I'm John Davidson, you can call me Jack."

She slapped it away. "Get that shit out of here, I'm a hugger."

Then she yanked me in and hugged me like I was her long-lost grandson just back from war. I didn't know what the hell to do, so I hugged her back, barely.

"That's not a hug! Are your arms broken?"

So, I squeezed a little tighter, still wondering what the hell was happening.

Who was this woman? Officer? Deckhand?

I knew I wasn't her relief. Jeff Fisher was the guy I was relieving. I've known him for over twenty years. We went through NUMI together, back in Groton.

So who the hell is she?

To my relief, she let go after four Mississippis once I adjusted my hug.

I stepped back, just out of her reach.

"Nice to meet you. That was quite a hello."

She smiled wryly and said, I swear, in a single breath, "Yeah, I know. You'll get used to me. I'm Rachel, by the way. I already have your bags. Smart of you to have your name embroidered on your seabags. Most people don't even carry seabags anymore. They show up with those stupid rolling suitcases. The wheels snap off as soon as they hit a steel deck. Total disaster."

While she talked, I made sure both seabags were accounted for.

When she finally gave me a second to speak, I said, "Thanks for grabbing both my bags," and then I followed up with the one question every sailor or mariner asks first, if you've ever worn a uniform, you're already saying it in your head:

"Where are you from, Rachel?"

\* \* \*

As we made our way to the van, her with one seabag, me with the other, Rachel gave me the Reader's Digest version of her life. Born and raised in Charleston, South Carolina. Joined the Navy right out of high school. Jumped to the Military Sealift Command after four years in uniform. She'd been on the HUDSON for six months.

During the five-minute ride from the air terminal to the pier, I gave her my own elevator bio. Retired Navy Chief. Independent Duty Corpsman. Submarines, then MSC for the past 6 years. Army brat. Born in Fayetteville, North Carolina. Currently living in

San Diego with my surprisingly patient wife of thirty years, Chloé.

As we pulled up to the pier, the HUDSON came into full view, port side to.

I knew she'd just come out of a maintenance period a month back, so I wasn't surprised to see her hull freshly painted. She looked almost fake, so clean and smooth it was like a plastic model floating on the water.

Then I looked up. The house, basically a steel apartment block stacked on the aft end with the bridge at the top, was another story. Rust spots everywhere. Unfortunately, that's Navy life. Different maintenance cycles mean not everything gets repainted at once. Still, the HUDSON was a beautiful ship, built to serve. And ready to go.

The gangway up to the main deck wasn't steep, a telltale sign the tanks were full. She sat lower in the water.

At the top, the watch stood behind a folding table with logbooks, a phone, and a manila envelope with my name on it.

The young guy took my orders and handed over the envelope in the same motion.

"Hey, Mark," he called. "Get over here and call the doc while I write this in the log."

As he scribbled, another mariner appeared from behind a weather shack, barely bigger than a phone booth. The guy looked like he'd rather be waterboarded than spend another minute on this ship. His duty shotgun hung from his shoulder, muzzle swinging freely...and right at my face.

Before I could say a word, Rachel lit him up.

"Goddamn it, how many times do I have to tell you, keep the barrel pointed at the deck! Carry that weapon like you've been trained."

He didn't say a word. Just adjusted the weapon, picked up the phone, and muttered,

"Hey Doc. Quarterdeck. New guy's here."

\* \* \*

I waited for Jeff to show up and take over as my escort.

Meanwhile, Rachel pulled the lackluster mariner somewhere out of sight and nearly out of earshot. I couldn't make out the words, but the tone and cadence came straight from the Unofficial Navy Chief Ass-Chewing Manual. With her breath control, I bet it was epic.

The manila envelope held the usual: a welcome-aboard letter signed by the captain, my job description, and the keys to my stateroom. Standard fare.

The main deck, also called the tank deck, was covered by the first deck but mostly open to the wind and sea outboard. As the name implies, this is where you access the fuel tanks. Nothing glamorous. Just pipes, valves, and the smell of diesel baked into steel.

A few minutes later, Jeff appeared, coming down a ladder not far from where I stood.

"What an ugly sight for sore eyes," he said, grinning. "I'm almost happier to see you than I'll be to see my wife and kids in a few days."

We gave each other the standard "bro" hug, one arm around a shoulder, the other delivering a back slap. It's so practiced among men that if we'd been in water, you'd have thought we were synchronized swimmers.

"Jeff, you haven't aged a day. You're still a wrinkly, old, smelly, fat bastard. And it saddens me that you're not lying about your wife and kids."

We laughed and walked off the tank deck. I carried both my seabags.

Unlike active-duty Navy ships, especially subs, MSC ships have at least one elevator. Thank God. Dragging two fully loaded seabags up five decks might've killed me.

Jeff and I are both Medical Services Officers, MSOs, but everyone onboard just calls us "Doc."

The MSO stateroom is designated by plan. I'd be moving into the same one I've had on every oiler I've worked.

Normally, the new Doc bunks in a temp room until the old one rotates out. But since we were in Diego Garcia, Jeff decided to move off early to the Gateway Inn, on his own dime.

That's what old friends do. And when old friends do something that generous, there's an unwritten law: the one who stays covers all meals and drinks until the other one's gone. I would've bought anyway.

Even though we've spent, at most, maybe twenty days together since graduating NUMI twenty years ago, we're still great friends.

Jeff walked ahead, jabbering about someone we both knew.

I lagged, dragging my seabags toward the port aft room on the fifth deck.

The floors were highly buffed, a good sign the steward staff knew what they were doing. Figures. Jeff probably had his foot firmly planted up their stern pipes. He's a great guy. I respect him a lot.

But our styles? Not exactly the same.

I've never been in this particular room before, but it feels like home.

Just inside the door, to the left, are two lockers with built-in dresser drawers. Straight ahead, a desk, bolted to the floor and built into the bulkhead. Above it, a bookshelf made for sea. The books sat behind a bar to keep them from dancing onto the deck in rough weather.

The bed was a double, bolted to both the deck and the bulkhead, directly across from the desk.

On the aft wall was a square window that didn't open. Looking out, I could see four decks down to the flight deck.

At the end of the lockers, tucked out of sight from the doorway, was the head, one toilet, one sink, and a metal walled shower with a plastic shower curtain.

Nothing fancy, but it had everything a Doc needs.

I turned back around and spotted the one thing that made this the official MSO stateroom: The call panel with five lights. One for each bed in the ward.

As I drop my bags on the bed, Jeff said, "Take a minute to settle, then meet me in the lounge."

I pull the toiletry kit from the top of one of the seabags and freshen up. You know, brush my teeth and wash my face. I dried my face with the 80-grit Navy-issue towel next to the sink.

Ah, fresh breath...and an exfoliated face. I figured I was ready to meet the captain.

\* \* \*

Foreword on the fifth deck, amidships, was the officer's lounge. Jeff was sitting there on the Naugahyde-covered couch sipping on a fresh-brewed cup of joe.

"You want a cup? I just made it."

It smelled good, no question. But I knew better, jet lag and all, I didn't need any help staying up tonight.

"No thanks buddy. Let's get this over with."

Jeff stood without a word. I did an about-face out of the lounge, and we climbed the forward stairwell, yes, MSC ships have stairwells, one deck up to the sixth.

Up there, the only spaces were the captain's cabin, cargo control, a VIP stateroom, and a bunch of fan rooms. I say 'only', when it's actuality a fair amount of space, but he's usually the only person on the sixth deck.

I was a little anxious to meet Captain Brown.

Not because I'd heard anything bad, I hadn't heard anything at all. Knowing a captain's reputation ahead of time lets you go in with a plan. If they're serious, you mirror it. If they're known to be affable, you stay professional, but a little looser. If they've got a Captain Bligh vibe, you ask yourself, How the hell did I piss off the detailers? And if Bligh is your cross to bear, you do your four-month rotation as quietly as possible and get the hell out.

He was standing behind his desk, looking out the window at the weather deck below, probably taking in the usual chaos.

Tall. Six-two. Dark wavy hair. Three days of stubble.

When Jeff knocked, he turned, and I saw the black T-shirt: Ernest Hemingway's face and the words Hog's Breath Saloon across the chest. Tan cargo shorts and OluKai flip-flops.

I think I'm going to like this captain.

Before Jeff could ask for permission to enter, the captain said, smiling,

"Get in here, you two, and have a seat."

The captain stepped out from behind his desk and shook my hand before we could even sit.

"John Brown, nice to meet you, Doc." His handshake was firm, but not aggressive. He wasn't trying to establish dominance; unlike some I'd met before.

"John F. Davidson," I said. "My friends call me Jack."

The meeting from there was uneventful, no need to relive it.

Fifteen minutes in he let out a yawn.

"Docs," he said, "that's enough of this bullshit."

He paused, measured me a little, then added, "Jeff here tells me you like a drink every now and then. You want to get out of here and experience the Diego Garcia Yacht Club?"

My brain was telling me the smart move was to get some rest.

Turnover with Jeff started in the morning. And honestly, my liver was still drying out from the free two-week vacation in Singapore.

What my mouth said was, "I'd love to."

\* \* \*

Welcome to Diego Garcia.

# Chapter 2—Diego Garcia

The implied "order" was to go drinking, and who was I to disobey an implied "order," even if it was dubious. Captain Brown told Jeff and me to change into atoll formal wear and meet him at the gangway in five minutes. My old bones moved as fast as they could. I was excited to see Diego Garcia, the Yacht Club especially.

Usually, I'm a bit of a Marie Kondo when it comes to an orderly room, but in my hurried state, I dumped one seabag out on the bed.

Crap, wrong one.

Then I dumped the other seabag. Bingo! Shorts, my version of the Ernest Hemingway / Hog's Breath Saloon shirt, and my OluKai flip-flops.

That thing I said earlier about mirroring, I had to stop a beat to wonder if I wasn't taking it too far.

Screw it. Even if I looked like a gigantic suck-up, this one was going to be a story told for years by Jeff. I was setting him up for a slam-dunk sea story. You know, the kind that starts with, this is a no-shitter.

The captain and Jeff were already at the gangway. Jeff saw my shirt first.

"Jesus Christ, Jack, brown-nosing the captain already?"

The captain turned, saw my shirt, and rolled his eyes. Not wanting to lose his captain-y air in front of the watch standers, he introduced me to the officer who was talking to her charges at the gangway folding table.

"Jack, this is Second Mate Janice Dillion, our navigator."

She was behind the folding table and extended her hand. "Nice to finally meet you."

I shook her hand and simply stated, "Jack Davidson."

Janice looked exceptionally young for her role – maybe 23 or 24, tops. I was about to start with the 'so where are you from' line when she beat me to the verbal draw.

"So you're the new doc. Jeff has been telling stories about you for weeks. Matter of fact, since he saw your orders, he hasn't shut up."

Jeff cocked his head, shrugged, and grinned. "I didn't want these fine folks to be blindsided by your obviously obnoxious style. They needed to be prepared for the shit-show that's about to befall them."

Captain Brown, growing tired of the banter, chimed in.

"Are you ladies going to blather on all night or are we going?"

Storytime was over.

\* \* \*

We followed the captain down the gangway and to his sedan, which was parked just forty feet away. Like a petulant child, Jeff sprinted for the shotgun seat, as if there was some advantage to the front seat of the car for a five or six-minute drive to the Yacht Club.

Sometimes I was surprised at how sophomoric we could be. Most of the time I gave us a pass because I understood well the pressure valve this behavior represented. Besides, sea stories usually don't just create themselves. They take creative thought and ingenuity. Try as we may, they don't all make it to sea story status. So, the volume of attempts is key to getting one that sticks.

I was wide-eyed for the drive. Jeff was spouting off locations as if I had the listening skills of a court reporter.

"To your right is the marina. Across the marina is the shore office for COMPSRON 2 – or as we used to know it, MSPRON 2. We used to have an MSO position there, but that ended a few years back."

By the time he got that complete sentence out of his mouth, we were already turning right.

Jeff continued, "This is the main drag on D-Gar. To your left are some military buildings, and to your right are more military buildings. You'll have nothing to do with any of them, so just note that you need to drive past them to get where you want to go."

In another blink of an eye: "These buildings on the left are housing for the non-military contractors that work just about every amenity on the atoll – the exchange, the Gateway Inn, the Chief's Club, the Officer's Club, on and on. If it wasn't for them, nothing would get done. And... they are mostly from the PI. We're not allowed to go down those streets. Strictly off-limits."

"To your right is the lagoon, where you can see all the prepositioned ships at anchor. They're anchored out because it's a blast radius thing – KA—BOOM!"

Jeff mimed the explosion with his hands and chuckled as if dying in a massive fireball would somehow be fun.

"Nothing to worry about. You'd only hear the KA."

Changing gears from morbid to let's-get-this-party-started, he immediately followed that with, "Brit Club. Yacht Club. Let's Drink."

* * *

The Yacht Club was a little short of pretentious. To the right was a walled room, about 20 x 20, if I had to guess. To the back left was a much smaller room that looked like it was where the supplies were stored. Between the two rooms was a concrete slab without

12

walls, approximately the same area as the two rooms combined. There was a bar with its back up to the storage closet room, and the concrete slab was surrounded by a wooden railing – I suspect to keep the drunks from falling that 1/2 inch vertical to the gravel parking area. Then over it all was a single roof. It was exceptionally charming for the middle of f'ing nowhere.

The first thing that caught my eye was all the men wearing red dresses. I'd like to say I didn't know what this was all about, but alas, I too had worn a red dress before. D-Gar being a British Territory, it made perfect sense that there was a Hash House Harriers club on the atoll, a drinking club with a running problem.

Before Captain Brown could get out of his sedan, a short, stocky guy wearing an ill-fitting kimono pulled the captain's door open and said, "We need to talk."

They disappeared out of sight. Jeff and me approached the club and because I knew the lingo, I yelled over the music, "On-in!"

The whole group yelled back in unison, "On-in!"

As soon as I set foot on the concrete, a fit, clean-shaven man – also in a red dress – handed me a Corona.

"I'm Commodore David Schwarzkopf, Governor of British Indian Ocean Territory, but while I'm at this event you can call me General Fuck Up."

"I suppose since you knew 'on-in,' that you're a hasher as well. What's your name?"

"Nice to meet you, General Fuck Up. I'm... Underwater Pecker Checker and this is my friend, Just Jeff."

He smiled. "Let me guess... you were at one time a corpsman on a submarine."

"Yep, you got me."

He turned to the crowd and yelled, "Hey everyone, this is Underwater Pecker Checker!"

Again, in near unison, "Hi, Underwater Pecker Checker!"

Just Jeff, 'Just' being the moniker for non-hashers, and I made our way to the bar. The female bartender handed him a beer without asking his order. He took a long draw and said, "This is the life. If you join the Diego Garcia Yacht Club, you're a member for life. You only pay what you want for drinks. And believe me, this place is flush with funds. Everybody has two or three beers that cost 50 cents wholesale and then slip $20 into the club fund."

The captain still hadn't appeared. As I was looking around for him, a cute girl in a red dress, dark hair pulled back in a ponytail, wedged her way in between Jeff and me. She had obviously been drinking for a while, and her accent was definitely British.

"So, you're Underwater Pecker Checker. It's a shame you like to play with male genitals, because my hash name is Whores d'oeuvre."

She giggled as she paused to let her hash name play in my head.

"I'm not a whore though, I'm a cook/baker and my specialty is hors d'oeuvres. I work at the Officer's Club. What brings you to this rock?"

Trying to divert her attention from me, I pointed to Jeff. "I'm his relief on the USNS Hudson. I just flew in today."

She looked at Jeff, looked at me. "Welcome to the island." And then disappeared as fast as a hummingbird at a feeder.

Jeff and I stayed at the bar for quite a while without sight of the captain. We swapped the same old stories. "Remember when Johnson dropped that carton of eggs..." "I nearly pissed my pants that time..."

14

Either one of us could have told the stories, but unofficial ownership of the stories over time had been decided. So, we told the ones we'd polished and listened to the ones we hadn't.

From time to time a curious person in a red dress would belly up and say their hellos. After a minute or two, they'd flutter elsewhere to talk with better-known mates.

I was starting to feel the alcohol when the captain reappeared. He wore the face of a man whose last beer was poured out on the ground by a smart-ass cadet. Jeff knew him. I felt it was his responsibility to ask about the sour look on his face.

"Hey Cap. You ok?"

He motioned with his head for us to get out of there. "We'll talk in the car."

Captain Brown walked like he was in a hurry, and Jeff and I, well, we tried to be in a hurry. It wasn't in the cards.

Once settled in the car, the captain said, "We were supposed to have two more weeks here for a little R-n-R and light maintenance, but now we have to head out in two days."

Jeff corrected, "YOU have to leave in two days. I'm staying right here until my flight."

The captain shot a look at Jeff. "Nice. Way to make everything about Jeff."

"Well, who else was I s'posed to make it about? I'm stayin' here. I feel bad for ya, cap'n, but it doesn't really affect me. I do, however, feel bad for you guys. I wanted to toss a few more back with you two. You know, smooth the transition to a new Doc. You know... because you're going to be so sorry the best damn doc you've ever known is leaving your ship. You'll need time to adjust to this peckerwood."

Captain Brown and I rolled our eyes at Jeff.

It only took a few minutes to get to Jeff's room at the Gateway Inn. Jeff stumbled out and then leaned back in the car.

"Buuuddy, I'll see you at breakfast tomorrow morning at 0730."

He shut the door and disappeared. I was left sitting in the back seat.

"Well, I'm not going to be your chauffeur. Get your ass up here."

I moved to the front seat and buckled in.

"Your buuuddy, Jeff doesn't hold his alcohol very well. Every port he's shitfaced. Was he like that when he was active duty?"

"I don't really know. I knew him in IDC school and there wasn't any time to get drunk. Fourteen hours a day, seven days a week, we studied. It was a meat grinder."

"Well, he's a lightweight when it comes to alcohol. Do you think you'll be able to turn over in the time we have left in port?"

"I've relieved Jeff once in the Navy and once in the MSC. His programs are tight. I'll count the narcs and look at his, correction, my, supply levels and then I'm good to go. Besides, Jeff is kinda organized. I'm a freak when it comes to organization. The Container Store calls me for organizing ideas."

He laughed. "Is that so?"

Second Mate Janice Dillion, the navigator, was still on duty when we arrived on the ship at 2330, standing right where we left her.

She announced to the watch stander, "Log the Captain and Doc 2 onboard."

"Captain, I was trying to reach you. I was getting a little worried. There was a message..."

He cut her off. "Yes, I saw your texts. Sorry, I didn't respond in a timely fashion. I got a little busy at the COMPSRON 2 office. Other than the schedule change message, anything else to report?"

"No, sir."

"Okay, set a department head meeting for 0900 tomorrow morning."

"Will do, Captain."

\* \* \*

I went up to my stateroom to find my very unorganized room. I didn't feel like dealing with the mess. I placed everything lumped on the bed into a pile in the corner. Sleep was more important than tidiness at this hour. I brushed my teeth, crawled exhausted into bed, and slept the sleep of the dead until jetlag hit and I woke at 0330.

I stared at the ceiling for an hour in an attempt to get on D-Gar time. It wasn't happening. I went outside to the smoking deck, which was a small weather deck just outside my stateroom. I don't smoke but I do enjoy better cell reception there than in my room. I FaceTimed my wife and we exchanged the usual "I miss you" and "Wish you were here". The reception was spotty, but I was happy to see her face and hear her voice. She knew Jeff and his wife from the submarine days, so she asked about them. As we said our goodbyes, she said, "Love you. Tell Jeff to behave himself." Fifteen minutes down, 2 hours and 45 minutes until breakfast.

Jeff gave me keys to sickbay, but I wasn't going to do anything there. The unspoken rule is: don't touch another doc's cabinets until the logbook says it's yours.

In high school I worked for McDonald's. Anyone who has ever worked there will tell you, "If you have time to lean, you have time to clean." Funny how that has stuck with me for 40 years.

The pile in the corner called to me. "Put me away. Fold me. I want to be hung." It all sounded so innocent until the dress shirt chimed in. How morbid.

\* \* \*

Jeff looked a little rough around the edges at breakfast, but I had to hand it to him, he showed up.

Sickbay looked good. Nothing too much to see. I've been in many of these sickbays. One thing for certain, everybody does it the same, but slightly different. As I had mentioned before Jeff and I don't organize the same. I don't organize to be a neat freak. The act of organizing creates muscle memory. I organize so I can act without thinking in an emergency. Everything in the same place every time – EVERY TIME.

I never wanted it said that someone died because I couldn't find a piece of gear. Hasn't happened yet, and God willing, it never will.

The narcotics were all in order. That's all I needed. Jeff had prefilled out the turnover letter, like a good MSO does, and we were ready for the captain's signature in an hour. This process usually takes two days, three if there's time.

At 0900 I joined a cast of unknown mariners in the fifth-floor lounge. The captain sat on the couch between, what I would later learn, were the Chief Mate and the Cargo Mate. He started almost immediately upon Jeff and me entering the space.

"I know the scuttlebutt has already started to fly. We were supposed to be on our way the NAG but plans have changed. The Rock has been delayed in the shipyard in Singapore. Therefore, there has been a drastic shuffling of the deck. New plan. We are now joining the USS Boxer and several other ships in the Banda Sea, for those not familiar, that's in the waters near Indonesia. The carrot here is two-fold. One, we don't have to go to the NAG..." The room quietly cheered. "And two, we might get a port call in Darwin, Australia."

There was a much louder cheer for the second carrot.

Captain Brown made hand gestures for the room to quiet down.

His attention turned to the Engineer, a.k.a. Eng.

"This means our last two days in Diego Garcia are going to be busy. Eng, you only have one thing on the maintenance list that might be an issue. Can you get that done before we leave?"

"No worries, Captain. I'll move two people on to that project and I'm certain with the extra manpower and some overtime, we'll have the head gasket replaced, tested, and we'll be ready to rock and roll."

He turned his attention to Jeff. "How's your turnover going?"

"Captain, I have the turnover letter ready for your signature right here in my hand."

He looked at us quizzically, "You two really pencil-whipped the hell out of that turnover."

I chimed in, "No sir. The narcs took five minutes to count, and this is the third time I've relieved the MSO. I know he runs a squared-away program, and I trust his numbers. Besides, we could spend three days turning over and here at the ass end of the world, there's nothing we could do about it, even if it was screwed up."

"Understood. See me in my office after the meeting and I'll sign the letter. It's yours now. You own it."

He called on each department head one at a time. None of them had anything urgent that would delay our departure.

In the captain's office there was no fanfare, just a signature and the weight that came with it.

* * *

Jeff became a ghost. He knew better than to hang around while I made the department my own.

We met at the Yacht Club the next two nights. The crowd was sparser than the red dress day and the number of beers consumed was too. Jeff regaled me with stories about what I was going to miss because my two-weeklong R-n-R stay in Diego Garcia was cut short. He told me about Turtle Cove, the wild donkeys, leftovers from the island's plantation days, the snorkeling, the Officer's Club Sunday Brunch, and all the other gems I'd be missing out on. He made the atoll sound like a Sandals all-inclusive resort.

One momentous occasion; I purchased my lifetime membership to the Diego Garcia Yacht Club and a Yacht Club bucket hat. You never know when I might be back on D-Gar and want to be treated like a long-lost friend.

The morning we departed, Jeff stopped onboard for one last free meal on the mess decks. Complain all you want about the chow, everyone showed up on burger day.

Jeff and I said goodbye. Not sure if or when we'd ever see each other again. We weren't sad, just two old buddies, long past expectations, glad for the time together.

We were scheduled to leave the pier at 1500 to coincide with the best tide. An hour before setting sail, all the key mariners gathered around the chart table on the bridge to hear the Navigator's departure plan. I'm not a required participant, but I'm a noisy SOB when it comes to ship's movements.

An hour later, at exactly 1500, I stood on the forward deck, watching the line handlers pull the last line on deck, the Mate on Watch announced over the loudspeaker: "1500, last line; ship is underway."

# Chapter 3—Banda Sea

Some days at sea drag. Others have more excitement than a heart should be able to bear, but we manage anyway. Most days settle into a mild kind of harassment with meals, coffee breaks, and cutting up with your shipmates. You know, a job.

My routine was simple. I opened sickbay for sick call twice a day. In the morning, right after breakfast from 0800—1000. In the afternoon, right after lunch from 1300—1400. During those hours my door stood wide open for all who needed me to enter.

During the rest of the day, I may or may not be in my office. I wore many hats. I monitored the water supply, inspected the food and the galley, conducted heat stress monitoring and on and on. There were 25 different jobs I performed, none of them overwhelming, but added together, it meant I needed to always be on my game.

The ship's main mission is to be a floating gas station and grocery store. USS Navy or NATO ships sail up beside us at sea, we attach to them with wires and hoses, and deliver the goods. An experienced crew made it look simple, but stand in the wrong spot when a line breaks or a span wire snaps, and it'll whip through a man like a hot knife through butter. I know the hot knife cliché is overused, but a hot knife does not move as fast through butter as a tensioned wire would travel through a man's body.

Sailing at a flank bell, making haste to the Banda Sea, there weren't any Underway Replenishments (UNREP) on the schedule. UNREPs were a love / hate relationship with the crew. It was our main mission, but it interrupted routine workflow. On the other hand, if the UNREP went past normal duty times, which it often did, it meant overtime. Everybody loves overtime. I know some mariners who had their regular pay direct deposited for their families and took cash advances to spend their overtime whenever we hit port. Sometimes the overtime pay was more than the regular pay.

Me, I got a hundred bucks a week. Agreed upon, not imposed. The rest went home. It wasn't a hardship. I'd do anything for Chloé and kids—yeah, I know, how original. If I really wanted something out here, I had high-limit cards and a wife who paid them. Don't cry for me. I do just fine.

* * *

Sailing with the MSC was different than the US Navy in a lot of ways. No real uniforms. No haircuts. Beard policy was flexible on some ships. I never cared about closely trimmed beards if they could get a seal on their respirators during a fit test. But the one thing that was tradition in the MSC that didn't happen in the active duty was coffee. Not the drinking of it, the scheduling of it. Every day at 1000 and 1500 was coffee. Not coffee break, not coffee time, it was simply coffee.

On my last ship the Engineering Department was the place to be for coffee. They damn near had a Starbucks in their control room. It was invitation only. Non-engineers could go pound sand. Two exceptions: the doc and the captain. You could set your watch to the captain and me showing up in Engineering Control for coffee. BAMM! 1000. BAMM! 1500. Of course, in every port me and the captain would go shopping for coffee supplies and turn them over to the engineering baristas.

To my great disappointment, the coffee mess in the engineer space on the HUDSON was crap. The first time I saw it I chewed them out for health violations. If they didn't clean it up by the following day, I threatened to secure it; that means shut it down. They cleaned up as demanded. I never returned to the engineer room for coffee.

My routine became morning coffee from the officer's mess and drinking it alone in my office while I continued to work. For afternoon coffee I would go to the bridge and have a cup with the captain and whoever else showed.

At least the coffee on the bridge was not the Navy issue brand. The deck officers and bridge watch standers chipped in for better coffees and cleaned their area. It didn't make me stop dreaming about the coffee on the USNS Used-to-sail.

The other thing about coffee is it wasn't just about the coffee. It was about learning your ship and your shipmates.

One day the conversation is deep and philosophical, the next you're telling fart jokes. When people are trapped on a tin can together the breadth of topics is important.

\* \* \*

At afternoon coffee Captain Brown and I began to get to know one another well. We were both born in North Carolina. As I mentioned, I was born in Fayetteville. He was born in Beaufort, for the uninitiated, it's pronounced Bo-fert. He came from a long line of fishermen and started his professional seafaring ways as a seaman recruit in the US Navy. He'd been away from Beaufort long enough that his southern drawl was faint. But if he got excited, boy-howdy, it came out thick!

We grilled each other about everything. It seemed no topic was off limits, though we talked in hushed tones if things we said were not for the ears of junior personnel.

When Second Mate Janice Dillion was on duty she would come over and chat with us as well. Unlike the other deck mates standing watch on the bridge, she didn't fear the captain. She showed due respect, but not an ounce of fear. Janice was exceptionally sure of herself for such a young person. She'd stand in there with us toe-to-toe, no matter the topic. I was most surprised when we talked about music, and she knew the soundtrack of my youth almost as well as I did. I took an instant liking to her.

The one thing that got her goat was how I would occasionally leave the 'I' out of her name.

"It's Dillion, Doc. There's an 'I' in there, Doc. Stop shortchanging me."

Janice was smart and tough. To further tease her, because that's what sailors do, I would mistakenly accuse her of graduating from the Massachusetts Maritime Academy instead of the Maine Maritime Academy.

"I'm not a Mass-hole, damn it."

Both those schticks got old fast, but it was fun while it lasted.

The more time I spent on the bridge, the more she showed her true self. She was tough as nails. She was also warm and funny. I sensed her bravado was real, but it was a survival technique she learned by excelling in male dominated field.

\* \* \*

Rachel Ryan darkened my doorway one morning.

"Hey, Doc. I haven't seen much of you around this first week onboard. Where you been hidin'?"

"I've been around. Mostly in here getting settled."

"Smells like you been cleaning. Smells like a sickbay should smell. Why haven't you been out on deck yet to visit us?"

"I've passed through. Without UNREPs during this transit there hasn't been much of a reason."

She looked at me, disappointed, "I'm not reason enough to visit the deck?"

I laughed because I knew she was yanking my chain. "I'll make sure to visit you on the deck sometime today. Where will I be able to find you and when?"

"I'll be in the mid-truck tunnel all day."

She looked like my aunt Shirley when she was thirty-something, which led me to ask, "You're from South Carolina, right?"

"Yeap, Charleston. You ever been?"

"Yeah, I've been to Detyens Shipyard in North Charleston a few times. I love that area...Hey, do you have any relatives in Missouri?"

"Not that I know of, why?"

"Well, you look a lot like my Aunt Shirley when she was your age. I thought we might be cousins ten times removed or something."

Without much thought she shot back, "You look kinda like my nephew if he was forty-five years older. My Doc, my nephew."

\* \* \*

On a T-AO oiler, there are tunnels on the first deck that allow for the transport of pallets. About half the area is open weather deck; the other half has three enclosed tunnels where fork trucks can pass through. The forward truck tunnel runs under the foredeck and provides access to supply and storage. The mid-truck tunnel includes open pallet storage, the bosun office, and the probe shop. The aft truck tunnel runs beneath the house, used for parking fork trucks and leading out to the flight deck.

I kept my promise and visited the mid-truck tunnel just before afternoon coffee. Rachel was in the bosun office with three other deck personnel, referred to as Able-bodied Seamen, or ABs.

Rachel quickly introduced me, "Hey guys, this is our new Doc, my nephew."

They looked puzzled. She continued to keep their heads spinning, "and I'm his Aunt Shirley."

And that is how endearing nicknames are born.

\* \* \*

At sea you should never complain that it's quiet. Sure enough, if you complain, King Neptune will hear it as a challenge.

We had sailed on peaceful waters for the first five days. Just as we were about to pass from the Timor Sea north into the Banda Sea, a storm blew in and rocked us for about twelve hours.

I was passing out seasick pills like M&Ms. Even the hardest, grizzled salts were asking for meclizine. Everyone, except essential watch standers, were told to stay in their racks. The evening meal was suspended because it wasn't safe for the galley crew. Besides, most everyone was nauseated.

I regretted not stocking up at the commissary in Diego Garcia. I found some fruit and peanut butter crackers in the fifth-floor lounge and counted myself lucky.

In these rough seas, laying down will help fight off seasickness but it won't keep you from getting bounced about your bed. A few waves had me hovering, but my tightly tucked sheets kept me from being thrown to the deck. The only other time I had experienced seas this rough, I was in a submarine, and we just dove a little deeper until it stopped. Not an option this time. We were on this roller coaster ride for as long as it was going to take.

About 0300 the worst of it was past. I was able to sleep for a few hours. At 0530 there was a knock on my stateroom door. I answered in just shorts.

It was Janice.

"Doc, the bridge woke me up and told me to get you. There's a small vessel capsized in the water with a person on top of it."

"Holy shit, I'll get dressed and head to sick bay."

"Captain wants you on the bridge first."

"Let me get dressed. I'll be right there."

She turned away and said, "Thanks."

I wasn't sure what she was thanking me for. Was it for doing my job or for getting dressed?

\* \* \*

The captain wanted my game plan and told me that we were about one hundred nautical miles from the USS Boxer, which had a complete medical staff onboard, including a surgeon.

"I'm almost certain he'll be hypothermic to some degree. Other than that, he can have anywhere from a scratch to shark bites. I just won't know until we get him onboard."

I thought for a second, "Who's going on the rib boat to get him?"

"I see that look in your eyes, it ain't going to be you. Don't even volunteer. Get the rib boat crew one of your EMAT bags."

Because the MSO was the only medical person onboard there was a small group on every ship assigned to the Emergency Medical Action Team (EMAT). Most had no medical training whatsoever, but if they were willing to learn, I could get them to be useful in a true emergency. Occasionally a fire would ignite someone's previously unknown interest. Several had become certified EMTs, and one real go-getter became a paramedic / firefighter.

The rib boat launched and retrieved without incident. A small man, soaked through and through, was helped out of rib boat on to the deck. He walked under his own power, shivering, but not as violently as I had anticipated.

The AB who jumped on to the capsized boat and assessed the man while in the rib on the way back to the HUDSON excitedly reported to me, "I didn't find anything wrong with him other than his skin feels cold."

I wrapped our guest in a pre-warmed blanket and escorted him to sick bay.

Once there he seemed to understand what was going on. I didn't even gesture for him to sit on the exam table and he jumped right up.

"How do you feel?"

He shook his head no and said something in a language I didn't understand, I assumed it was Indonesian.

I asked, "Indonesian."

"Indonesia", he said with a smile. He placed his hands together as if in prayer and bowed his head. "Terima kasih."

I placed my hand on my chest and said, "Jack Davidson."

He mimicked me and said, "Ahmad Khong."

I showed Ahmad the thermometer and mock-put it in my mouth and pointed at him. He opened his mouth. Grunts and gestures will do in a pinch. What I really needed was his core temperature, but I wasn't sure how to gesture that best practice in this situation dictated a rectal temperature. Oral will have to do.

Thankfully his oral temperature was 95.8°F. Low but not too dangerous.

A cook knocked on the door. "I have coffee or tea for your patient."

Ahmad understood and reached for the tea.

A beat later the captain arrived, "How's he doin', Doc?"

"I think he's lucky. So far all I can tell is his temp is low. But he'll be fine. I still need do perform a more thorough exam."

The captain slapped me on the back, "Get him cleaned up and in some fresh clothes. I just got off the phone with the Boxer. They're sending a helo. They're trying to arrange a transfer to a civilian hospital somewhere on one of these Indonesian islands. According to the Nav, Yamdena is closest. Helo ETA is about two hours."

I finished the exam. Other than still shivering, Ahmad was the picture of health.

In the ward, there was a head and shower. While he was in the shower, the supply team brought him some new coveralls, underwear, boots, and socks they had in storage. The ship's store operator gave him a ship's hat and a ship's T-shirt. The rest of the crew donated over $200 so he'd have funds to deal with whatever awaited him once he got ashore.

He dressed and I took his temperature again. 97.2°F. He was recovering well.

I motioned to my mouth to see if he was hungry. Yes, he was.

It just so happened to be breakfast time. He was able to make his choice from a wide variety of foods. Rice, scrambled eggs, and more tea was his choice. With all his new clothes Ahmad looked like a crew member as we sat on the mess decks eating.

The helo arrived. A quick picture in the aft truck tunnel with a few of the crew and he was on his way.

He won't forget about getting fished out the water by an American supply ship. We certainly won't forget about our two-hour shipmate, or how we came together, off script, to save a life.

* * *

The weather cleared. The sea returned its normal state of small swells and a few white caps.

The crew was slightly upset, we were supposed to perform a crossing the line ceremony, the ancient tradition performed when crossing the equator. The storm set us behind schedule. Mission before fun. All pollywogs would have to wait to become shellbacks.

I donned my UNREP gear. On my head was a white hard hat emblazoned with a red cross. A white floatation vest, also emblazoned with a red cross on the back, protected me from an accidental trip over the gunwale. The final piece of personal protective equipment (PPE) were steel-toed boots, without any red crosses. Near the bosun office in the mid-truck tunnel, I placed my rapid response bag, you guessed it, emblazoned with a red cross.

My job during an UNREP was safety observer, aka the command voyeur. If I touched anything related to the actual performance of the UNREP, I would be reprimanded by the Cargo Mate or the Bosun. There were several others on the deck supervising what was going on as well, but they were involved in the process, so the theory was, the MSO was outside the process and could watch without developing a bias towards the process. For me it meant finding people who were resting and checking that they were still mentally and physically in the game.

A US frigate approached us on the starboard side, and we were going to transfer fuel to them. A process that would take about 2 hours.

First the ships' bridges established communications and they matched speeds. When the word was given, a shrill whistle was blown, and they shot a rifle at us. The projectile was about the size of an 8oz glass made of solid rubber. It wouldn't kill you. You'd notice if it hit you. Attached to the projectile was a thin red string called shot line. The shot is attached to slightly larger line, which is attached to a slightly larger line, which is attached to a slightly larger line, which is attached to the span wire.

The frigate attached the span wire to their ship and then we put tension on the wire at about 10,000 lbs, taut enough for a circus performer to walk between ships or support the weight of the fuel hoses, which is what we did with it. Next, we'd send the probe and fuel lines across. Then the fuel would be transferred through the fuel lines. It was just like a gas station, but it took two hours to fuel. Larger ships could take up to twelve hours to fuel.

Over the next four days we performed this delicate dance on the sea ten times. Lines go over. Span wire goes over. Fuel goes over. Lines come back. Span wire comes back. Set up the station and repeat. The overtime was flowing. The crew was happy. Everything was working well.

\* \* \*

On the fifth day the USS Boxer was our customer. They are a big ship and they take a lot of fuel, both diesel fuel marine (DFM) and jet fuel (JP-5). After all the other customers, the Boxer was going to bleed us nearly dry. That meant two things; we were going to be riding higher in the water and we were going to have to get to port to get more fuel.

Fueling the Boxer was a long day. They approached us on the port side. Everything went well until the span wire at Station 8 was tensioned. As it reached full tension there was a pop. Everyone hit the deck. The span wire was still there, but nerves were fried. An emergency breakaway was called. All tension in the wires dropped and the wires were quickly released into the water. The Boxer veered away from us. We reeled the wires back onboard. As the hook at the end of the wire cleared the surface of the water there was a fishing net looped around the hook.

The Cargo Mate, Matt Bartholomew, was looking over the gunwale and started yelling "Turtle! Turtle!"

This wasn't a normal command. Everyone was confused. Then a second person on the deck started yelling, "There's a turtle in a net!"

The command was given to get the turtle on the deck as fast as we could.

On Station 8 was the largest sea turtle I had personally ever seen. Lying on its back with a net tightly wrapped around its left hind flipper. As soon as the crew saw the wound beneath where the net was wrapped, everyone started calling for me, "Doc, Doc, you gotta get over here. This turtle needs medical attention."

I was dumbfounded. I don't remember a class at NUMI entitled turtle health. Flesh is flesh. I was sure the same principles applied.

The bosun got in there before I could. She drew a knife from her waist and with a few strokes freed the turtle from the net.

The turtle, which had been motionless up to this point, started flapping all its flippers wildly. If something was trying to eat it, the turtle was going to get in some licks first.

As soon as it calmed down, I got in there to take a look. The wound was mostly healed. In a few spots the scab had opened but there wasn't any serious bleeding. I took a 4x4 gauze pad, soaked in betadine and wiped the wound. I don't know why he started flapping again. I was using my softest patient care voice. My turtle bedside manner was impeccable.

I decided there wasn't anything else I could do. One smartass in the crowd suggested we make turtle soup. He was quickly booed and then playfully pummeled by his friends.

The only thing left was to put the turtle back in the sea.

Three hundred pounds was the consensus guess for the turtle's weight. Six of us slid the turtle onto a flattened tri-wall box. The turtle began to flap its flippers again. It was not an easy lift. Turtle flapping. Mariners unsteady on their feet. I was doing the odds in my head, what was the over/under on the number of mariners joining this turtle in the ocean? I'd set the line at one. Thankfully the under would have paid. The turtle landed in the water with a loud "TWACK!", and he was gone.

For the second time in a week this crew came together to save a life. One we pulled from the sea, one we returned to it. As I always say, "A place for everything and everything in its place."

* * *

With the turtle drama finished, the crew turned its attention back to the UNREP. We still needed to figure out the issue with Station 8 and start servicing the Boxer.

The issue at Station 8 couldn't be solved to anyone's satisfaction. The UNREP had been delayed for three hours. It was decided we were switching sides. The Boxer would now be on our starboard side. Station 1 would send JP-5 and Station 7 would send DFM.

This time the UNREP went off without a hitch, though it didn't end until 2300. Thankfully when the deck crew was setting up the starboard side they realized the UNREP would run into the darkness.

When that happens, everything gets glow sticks attached to it. Hard to see the fuel lines and people at night without glow sticks. And if you've been on the deck for 14 hours, with the hoses bouncing around at night, and if you squint just hard enough, and if you're just bored enough, the glow sticks look like they're having a midair rave party.

Once the UNREP with the Boxer was secured. The entire deck crew dragged their tired bones into the house to dream about our upcoming port visit to Darwin.

The trick was on us. The plans had been changed. We were heading to Guam. Oh, the disappointment the crew was going to feel when they found out over breakfast.

# Chapter 4—Guam, U.S.A.

Guam is an unsung jewel in the American Crown. Won as part of the spoils of the Spanish-American War, and except for a brief period during World War II, a territory few Americans know much about.

The island isn't very big, thirty miles north to south and eight miles at its widest. As one of my favorite movie characters, Dudley Moore's Arthur, would say, "It's s-m-all. It's so small, Rhode Island could kick the crap out of it." Yep, Rhode Island, the United States' smallest state, is six times bigger than Guam.

Here's what sets Guam apart: the Chamorro. They are not Polynesian like Hawai'ians. They are Austronesian. But just like their Hawai'ian, do I dare say, cousins, they are struggling to keep their culture and language alive during an onslaught of immigrants from the US and nearby Asian countries.

Arriving in Guam was like coming home. 'Hafa Adai' Guam.

\* \* \*

I was stationed here when I was on active duty, and I have many fond memories of the island. None was as vivid as the memory of approaching the island from the West and entering Apra Harbor.

To take advantage of the 'feels' I was having returning to Guam, I wanted to observe our entry into Apra Harbor on the starboard bridge wing with the captain and the Chief Mate, Theodore "Teddy" Stone at their arrival posts.

Among unique characters, Teddy stood out. You've heard of the term 'larger than life'? Teddy was larger than two. The deck department loved his sayings, 'Be a Viking today', and how he always had their backs. He was quick to laugh and just as quick to pull you up by your collar if you weren't holding up your end of the deal. He worked hard and, when he decided to play, he played even harder.

The thing that struck me most about Teddy was, he had one of the hardest jobs on the ship, but he never seemed to want to take the next step to captain. His saying about being a Viking wasn't fake. He wanted to be in the fight. He wanted dirt under his fingernails. He loved his guys on the deck and that's where he wanted to be. The captain could love his crew, but he had to maintain a little distance. Call it the air of command, or whatever. That just wasn't Teddy.

When I walked out on the starboard bridge wing the captain and Teddy both looked to see who had arrived. The harbor pilot, who stood next to the captain directing our movements and coordinating with the tugboats, was too busy to care who had just arrived.

Teddy spoke up, "So, Doc. You finally decided to come up here to do some real work."

I just nodded, you know, s'up style.

"Have you ever been to Guam, Doc?"

"Yes, I have. You?"

"Nope. First time. I was always an East Coast / Med sailor until I came to the Huddy in the shipyard in Singapore."

I smiled because I had all the information and a rare chance to actually dominate a conversation with Teddy.

"To our starboard is Orote Point. As you can see, it stands about 100 feet above the water. On the side facing us is the Spanish Steps. They lead down between those two rocks, there." I pointed near the westernmost part of Orote Point. "In between the rocks is a shallow, protected area of water. It's always warm, like a bathtub."

"See how it's flat on top? That's a World War II airfield. The US and Japanese both used it. It sits unused today."

I pointed further inland.

"That pier over there is the Kilo pier. It's used for explosive handling. Far away from the population. Duh, like I need to explain the concept of explosive arcs to you."

"Next, is that large beach area. That's Gab Gab beach. If you scuba dive, you can enter the water there and swim to some of the best coral reefs on the island. The best part is this is all on the Navy base. The worst part is it's within the explosive arc of the Kilo pier, so it gets closed regularly."

"Looking to port, you'll see the breakwater that was built by the SeaBees during World War II. Before that Apra Harbor was open to the sea. At the end of the breakwater, you see all those fuel tanks?"

Teddy nodded yes.

"Two or three of those fuel tanks were set ablaze during Typhoon Pongsona in 2002. I sat sheltered, right over there, and watched them burn for hours. It was the weirdest thing watching 150 mph winds whip the orange flames into the sky. It was a tragedy, but it was beautiful too. I don't remember anyone dying, but the island was a mess. No gas, no fresh water, no electricity. It took some parts of the island six months to get electricity. Took longer than that to get back to normal."

I always tried to be an observant visitor on the bridge, but I guess the excitement of telling the Chief Mate about Guam sidetracked me. With diplomatic restraint, Captain Brown ended the conversation by simply asking Teddy a work-related question.

My audience had been taken from me. Teddy gave me a quick wink, and the moment passed. I left the bridge to take in the rest of our arrival from the foredeck.

* * *

The tugs led us to Victor Pier and gently nestled us in, port side to. The first line went across and we were officially in Guam. Until a line attaches a ship to the pier it is technically still underway.

Unlike in Diego Garcia the gangway was not amidships. This time the flight deck lined up with a two story on the pier and the gangway bridged the gap. That meant the quarter deck was in the aft truck tunnel.

I just happened to be in the aft truck tunnel when the ship's first visitor arrived. I didn't recognize him, but he knew me immediately. "Hey, Doc! What the hell are you doin' here?"

I studied him for a second trying to think where I knew him from. As the memory hit me, he said, "John Freeman, from the USS Georgia."

"Hell yes, it's you. Last I saw you was in Bangor, Washington almost twenty years ago. It took me a second to reconcile you being in Guam. Do you live here?"

"Nah, I'm with the MSCPAC out of Pearl Harbor, HI. I'm just here for a quick job in the engine room. I traveled with the part." He patted the pelican briefcase he was carrying. Then he lifted his left pant leg.

"Remember this?"

A V-shaped scar ran from just below his kneecap to just above his ankle.

"Yeah, I remember that. I still have back pain from leaning over you in that tiny sick bay on the GEORGIA. How long did it take me to stitch you up? Eight hours?"

"Yeah, something like that."

Yes, I stitched John up and yes, he was an old shipmate. Truth be told, we never hung out in the old days. I still felt obligated to ask him to dinner.

"Wanna hit the town later? We could get a bite to eat and drink a few beers while we relive Captain Cooper stories."

He was gracious in his refusal. "I'd love to, Doc. But I'll be here all evening getting this part installed and then I have a flight back home early tomorrow morning."

"OK, it's been nice seeing you. I just have one more question for you. What's my name?"

That was my old gag on the submarine. The old Rumpelstiltskin I called it.

"Oh, not that shit again!" John laughed. "You know damn well I don't know your name. What's your name Doc? I'll remember it this time."

I smirked, "It's Jack Davidson, but you won't remember this time either. It's ok. I like the name Doc better anyway."

We shook hands and he started towards the engine room. "Same old, Doc, we'll see you around."

I knew another chance meeting with John Freeman was highly unlikely, but I said, "Yeah, see you around."

\* \* \*

By 1600 I had completed all my arrival duties. I was excited to get off the ship because it was Wednesday and that meant it was almost time for the Wednesday Night Market at Chamorro Village.

I changed into my official Guam wear: board shorts, a flowery, buttoned-up shirt, and my OluKai flip-flops. Though on Guam they're not called flip-flops, they're zori, the Japanese term for sandals.

I went up to the sixth deck to see if Captain Brown wanted to join me at Chamorro Village. Teddy and Janice were also there.

I knocked and entered, "Hey, do you guys want to go the Wednesday Night Market?"

Teddy replied, "Captain was telling me about it earlier today on the bridge. That's where we're heading. You can join us."

The Chamorro Village was just as I remembered it. Lots of crafts and artisans and food. Oh, the food! The smells from all the grills were Pavlovian; meat, smoke, and spice curling through the air until your stomach answered on instinct.

About half the space was dedicated to pop-up food stalls. The first round I went straight Chamorro – kelaguen and red rice. Second round I switched to Filipino food – lumpia and pancit. I topped all that off with a couple of beers and I was ready to explode, both physically and with joy.

The others weren't shy about stuffing themselves either. For Teddy and Janice, this was their first experience with such cuisine. They enjoyed it almost as much as I did.

\* \* \*

The next two nights Captain Brown and Teddy weren't available to go out. Janice and I had kind of established ourselves as liberty buddies, so we went out to dinner in Tamuning both nights. Once to the Hard Rock Café and the second night to a steakhouse.

At the steakhouse Janice said, "This place is so fancy. We're wearing nice clothes. This almost feels like a date."

My eyes just about fell out of my head. She noticed my expression immediately.

"Oh, get over yourself old man. I didn't say we were on a date. I said...almost feels like a date. Besides, eww. My father is younger than you."

I laughed with relief, "Thank God, I was about to have a heart attack."

I reached across the table and held her hands, time to do the mariner thing and turn the awkwardness in her direction.

Janice's eyes widened, her nostrils flared, and her mouth gaped open.

In the sweetest voice I could muster I said, "Janice, I know we just met not that long ago, but would you like...to...be...my...work daughter."

To my surprise she didn't double down. Her answer was sincere, "Yes. I will be your work daughter. You kind of remind me of dad."

And just like that, an attempt at playing the mariner game turned heartfelt.

My wife and I only had sons and she had always wanted a daughter.

To seal the unofficial adoption, I called the waiter over to take our picture and immediately text the picture to my wife with the caption – 'you always wanted a daughter. This is Janice. Can we keep her?'

It was early morning in California, but her reply returned almost immediately. 'Yes.'

Nobody knew my silliness better than my wife.

I showed Janice the texts. "I guess it's official now, Doc."

After that night at the steakhouse, things between Janice and me didn't change in any drastic way. We still had snarky comments for each other, but they were softer. We didn't start hanging out more. We didn't tell the crew anything, but we both knew deep down that we were there for each other, no questions asked.

The next day on the HUDSON the deck around Station 8 was a mess. The span wire was completely removed from its spool. It laid about the deck like a big pile of spaghetti. Greasy ABs were everywhere. Turns out the noise that puckered everyone's stern tube, was a single frayed strand in the wire. We were lucky during that UNREP with the USS Boxer. In Navy Safety parlance it's called a near miss, a disaster that could have happened but didn't.

Thankfully we carry extra span wire onboard for just such an occasion.

* * *

While the deck department dealt with their mess, I had my own dragons to slay. I was busy getting medical requirements completed. People needed hearing tests and physical exams. Because the ship's schedule is always in flux, it's nearly impossible to make plans before arriving in port.

The MSC is the civilian supply arm of the US Navy. Therefore, when available, the US Navy provides services to complete Navy mandated exams. Not every Naval Hospital understood this relationship or the complexity of delivering these services on short notice.

At the Naval Hospital Guam, I had a secret weapon. Her name was Estelle.

Estelle was a five foot nothing, Filipina and Chamorro, ball of energy. She walked fast, talked fast, typed fast. Landing in her sphere was like getting sucked into a tornado. The irony is that with her operational speed being what it was, you'd think she wouldn't have time to be personable. Nope. She was as sweet as North Carolina tea.

My routine was to send an email with my requests to Estelle as soon I had confirmation that we were heading to Guam. I don't exactly know how she performed her magic for me, but she rarely failed. Something tells me, because of her short stature, that she just might be a real fairy and uses pixie dust to charm all the doctors.

However she performed her magic, it was unique to her. In all the Navy Hospitals I've worked with around the world, there was only one Estelle.

* * *

By Sunday, my work was humming along and the deck department had Station 8 almost back in service, at least all the dangerous acts like climbing the king posts were over. It felt like time for a day outing. Going out for dinner and drinks after work gets stale when it's every day.

Back in my Guam days, I golfed, A LOT. Unfortunately, that never translated to any meaningful gain in skill. What it did teach me is that the golf courses on Guam were the attraction, not just the game. In the south the courses featured the mountains. On the east side of the island the Pacific Ocean was the draw. If you wanted a flatter more open course, you golfed in the north of the island in Dededo.

For me the best course was on the east in Mangilao. I called to reserve a tee time. Now all I needed was three more players.

Nobody wanted to join me. Teddy made a snide remark about it not being a real man's sport. Janice didn't golf. Rachel laughed in my face. I was getting desperate. I asked the Cargo Mate, Matt Bartholomew. Thankfully he said no. Then I found Captain Brown down in engineering room control (ERC) chatting with the Chief Engineer, Samuel Smith. They both said yes.

Using rented clubs, we set out to remove the topsoil of the Sono Felice Country Club one divot at a time.

We did the tee toss method to see who would ride in the golf cart solo. The tee pointed to the captain. The Eng and I loaded our clubs on our cart and off we went to the first tee.

"Doc, you're relatively new here, so I need to tell you something. Out here you call me by my first name. I don't want to hear any of this 'sir' BS."

"Aye, Aye Captain."

He shot me a look. "John, in case you forgot."

I turned to the Eng, "What do you prefer? Samuel or Sam."

In his subdued Texas drawl, "You can call me anything you want. If I know you're talkin' to me, I'll answer."

"Shithead it is."

John spit his beer out and coughed.

Sam laughed, "Well, maybe not that."

The round was going well. Nobody was about to give up going to sea to seek their pro tour card, but some nice shots were made. Sam sunk a 60-foot, double break, prayer of putt.

In between shots Sam and I got to know each other. He was from Houston, Texas. Son of an oil executive. His interest in the sea came from his uncle, a career Navy man, who filled his head with sea stories. Out of high school he applied to Annapolis and because someone told him not to put all his eggs in one basket, he also applied to the Massachusetts Maritime Academy. Mass Maritime is where he ended up.

"So, you're a Mass-hole."

"Nope. I'm a Texan. I never bought into all that academy false bravado BS. I measure people by how they perform at sea. You can have the best pedigree imaginable, but if the dog don't hunt."

Truer words were never said.

The whole reason I wanted to golf in Mangilao unfolded before us as our golf cart cleared the trees. Hole number 12. It doesn't have the attention of famous holes like Torrey Pines, Pebble Beach, or Augusta, but I'd put number 12 up against any hole in the world for the beauty and awe it inspires.

A par three, the tee box is on one side of a cove and about 127 yards away is the green perched on a small peninsula that juts out into the ocean. To the right of the tee box along the shoreline, is a fairway for scared golfers to lay up and approach the green from land.

The surf comes straight towards the elevated tee box. As you approached your ball, the waves lap the shore ten feet below. Your sightline to the green is backdropped by the Pacific Ocean. The experience is spiritual.

John and Sam reacted exactly as I had hoped. They feel it too.

Dinner was along the east coast as well, away from the bright lights and tourist traps in Tamuning. Jeff's Pirates Cove in Ipan offered a cool beach bar feel. It was a come-as-you-are, relaxing meal, looking out over the ocean. We ate quietly. The round of golf had sapped us of our energy.

\* \* \*

Our orders were to leave Guam on Tuesday. So that meant at 0600 Monday we were shifting to the Delta Pier and filling our tanks.

Since our tanks were essentially dry, Monday was going to be a very long day. The shore folks hooked us up at 0900 and pumped fuel for 14 hours. The ship settled in the water inch by inch as the day wore on.

While part of the department dealt with the fuel, the other half loaded cargo, mostly food and some repair parts for the ships we'll rendezvous with in a few days. The refrigerator and freezer Conex boxes on deck were filled to maximum capacity. The forward and mid-truck tunnels were stuffed with palletized items. The once open deck was an obstacle course with fork trucks whizzing about. Keeping your head on a swivel was a must.

At 1000 Tuesday morning I stood on the foredeck chatting with Rachel as the last line from the Delta Pier was brought on board. We were underway. Once again, I was saying goodbye to Guam. Was this the last time or would I be back? I don't know, the wind is in control.

# Chapter 5—Philippine Sea

Past the breakwater the HUDSON turned right and headed north to the Philippine Sea, where six ships awaited her over an eight-day period. One was a fellow MSC ship, the USNS Doris "Dorie" Miller (T-AKE 18), named after a mess attendant on the USS West Virginia who manned an anti-aircraft machine gun during the attack on Pearl Harbor despite never having been trained on the weapon. For his bravery, he was the first African American ever awarded the Navy Cross.

\* \* \*

When larger ships have helicopters there is another dimension to underway replenishment known as vertical replenishment, or VERTREP. Pallets are loaded into cargo nets (slings) and a helo hovers low enough for two of our crew members to hook the cargo to the helo using a cargo hook, but it's no easy task. It's akin to threading a needle in a hurricane. On a T-AKE class ship, it's not unusual to send over a hundred pallets this way–two or three pallets at a time.

For the pilots of the helos it's like being a hummingbird. They flit to and fro, picking up slings and dropping them off. For the flight deck crew, hooking the helo isn't just physically hard, it takes nerves of steel. Some pilots are better than others. Sometimes the helo gets too low and we gasp in horror, thinking we're about a second away from watching two of our shipmates get crushed. It's never happened that I know of, but it could. Helos aren't famous for their aerodynamics.

Here's the kicker—it happens all the time without incident. The hard becomes routine. For those who have done it a thousand times it can be boring, just another chore to get through.

Besides special nerve and skill, working on the flight deck requires special PPE. The float coats and cranials are flight deck approved. When performing both evolutions at the same time, I kept two sets of PPE on standby and switched between them as I bounced back and forth between VERTREP and UNREP. The other addition to flight quarters, as it's called when we're set up for a VERTREP, a helo firefighting team is standing by, dressed at 'half-mast'—pants and boots on, tops and hoods off.

The first two ships we serviced were UNREP and VERTREP combined. One team mans the flight deck and another team mans the fuel station. Sometimes we have multiple fuel lines going across the water to the same ship. It all depends on whether they're receiving just DFM or both DFM and JP-5. Both products can be delivered simultaneously via separate hoses.

Not every UNREP or VERTREP is exciting, thank God. When things get exciting at sea it's something like, 'Holy shit, Timmy's on fire.' And nobody likes Timmy on fire, especially Timmy. To reiterate, boring good.

Exciting bad.

* * *

The next day we were the lead ship with an UNREP with the MILLER. To be the lead ship is like taking the lead in a dance, you're both there, practically in the same space, but someone must coordinate the

49

movements so there's no awkward hull-on-hull contact.

In simplest terms, the HUDSON is a fuel ship with some capacity for cargo, the MILLER is a cargo ship with some capacity for fuel. They had some cargo to give us for a customer, and we had enough fuel to replenish their smaller tanks.

The other big difference is that MILLER and all T-AKEs have their own helicopter detachment onboard. Two Pumas to be exact, piloted mostly by retired Navy pilots. It might not even be an exaggeration that these gentlemen have more flight time than the combined active-duty fleet. (OK, that was a gross exaggeration, point made). Some of the newly trained active-duty pilots were a little jerky on the stick. I've seen our crew members hit the flight deck in self-preservation more than once under a CH-60. The Puma pilots were so smooth, you could tie a tea bag under them, and they could repeatedly dip it in a cup of hot water. Ah, Earl Grey.

During this evolution we received cargo and they received fuel. One piece of cargo they brought to us was a new bosun. It's not that Rachel wasn't doing the job, she was, but she was a bosun mate, temporarily filling the bosun position. I was on the flight deck when the new bosun arrived. He was dressed in flight ops PPE when he stepped off the helo, all I saw of him was his height. I figured I'd meet him later when he came to medical to check-in.

* * *

VERTREP and UNREP complete. The ship settled back into its regular routine. It's time for afternoon sick call, so I'm sitting in my office just doing whatever it is I do, and Rachel walks in to introduce the new bosun.

The first thing I notice is the finely trimmed mohawk he's sporting. Sunglasses are nestled on top of his head, the mohawk acting like non-skid, keeping them in place. He's about an inch taller than Rachel. That doesn't make him short, Rachel is just that tall. The sleeves are cut out of his coveralls and his tan arms are buff with a stereotypical sailor woman tattooed on his left forearm. She's standing tall, looking over her shoulder, wearing a Dixie cup sailor hat, looking proud of her cartoonishly heart-shaped rear.

Rachel says, "Nephew, this is the new bosun, Nigel Pavlavan."

Nigel looked puzzled.

Rachel explained. "I'm his Aunt Shirley, so that makes him my nephew."

This explanation did nothing to solve the riddle for Nigel.

Since he was already mixed up, I thought, let's really lean into this.

"Yup, we're related, and our family motto is incest is best."

I thought I'd get a laugh. The good news is Nigel no longer looked confused. The bad news is he now looked concerned.

"Ah, that's my wife you're talking about."

I nearly drew mud.

Rachel laughed at my discomfort. Maybe it was a set up, but who could have predicted the idiotic babble that spewed from my mouth. Not me, I'm always surprised by it.

"I'm sorry, it was just a joke." Then Rachel and I co-told the story of how she became Aunt Shirley.

He must have sensed by unease and gave a wry smile. "Relax. I believe you."

I sighed with relief, "Welcome aboard."

Nigel was in on the joke now and I lived to embarrass myself with many ill-timed, bad taste jokes for years to come.

\* \* \*

The salt of the sea wears at everything all the time. It never takes a day off. The other issue with ships is that machines are run 24 hours a day for weeks and months at time. Maintaining a ship is a constant battle and no matter how hard you fight against it, the best you can do is break even for a second. As soon as you turn your back, the sea starts tearing at your work.

There are other times when Naval regulations need to be upheld for safety reasons.

After finishing the last of our UNREPs for this trip at sea, a message was received from MSC headquarters. Our Aqueous Film-Forming Foam (AFFF) was expired, and we couldn't be at sea without it. Even though we had a full tank of AFFF, it automatically stopped working at 0001 on the designated expiration date.

The fix? Get to Sasebo, Japan, immediately and wait for instructions.

We turned north once again and slipped between the Ryukyu Island chain into the East China Sea.

A day later at 0800 we were at the opening to Kujukushima Bay. We slowed our approach because with larger ships like ours it was too narrow for them to exit and enter simultaneously. A large LPG ship passed to our port side, and now it was our turn.

Third Mate Scott Barlow was the Mate on Watch. He had all the experience in the world around him, Captain Brown, Teddy, Janice, the Japanese pilot, but he was responsible for the ship.

The pier we would eventually go to wasn't ready for us. To begin our stay in Sasebo we were going to be anchored out in the bay in a designated area, out of the shipping lanes.

The bay is surrounded by low mountains or high hills. Not sure which is the correct description here, for consistency I'll say mountains. Anyway, the mountains surrounded the bay, giving it a bowl-like appearance. Our anchor point was about a 1/4 mile from the shore.

Scott Barlow had performed perfectly up to this point. He was unaware of the problem he faced. The captain knew better. Being the wise and gentle teacher that he was, the captain, standing only two feet from Scott, leaned towards him and said in a voice barely above a whisper—

"You going to park this pig halfway up that hill or do you want me to take over."

Scott hadn't accounted for his speed. Four knots may not sound like much, unless you're trying to stop 42,000 metric tons of steel in a half mile of water.

In the category of 'knows the right answer when slapped in the face with it', Scott responded, loud and clear, "Captain has the con."

Without emotion, the captain said, "All back full."

The engine room responded. The ship stuttered with the change in propeller and the HUDSON reacted just as the captain wanted. She stopped right on the mark. "Drop anchor."

And with that, our unscheduled stay in Sasebo, Japan began.

# Chapter 6—Sasebo, Japan

The breasting barge is tied starboard side amidship under the ship's gangway ladder. The gangway is lowered onto the barge and then we access the liberty boat via the barge. Quite simple and effective.

The liberty boat has a wheelhouse that sits forward atop the main seating area which is enclosed and can hold twenty mariners. Behind the wheelhouse is an open seating area that seats a dozen more mariners. The stern has room for two or three mariners to stand and smoke.

The pilot was assisted by a single deckhand. Though the foot holds and hand holds weren't ample; the deckhand moved about the liberty boat with ease.

When the liberty boat approached the breasting barge, the deckhand appeared from the wheelhouse and moved forward to the bow of the boat. With speed and nonchalance, he lassoed a cleat on the barge and tightened it down. He tiptoed along a one-foot-wide deck that was outboard of the enclosed passenger area to the stern of the boat. He tossed another line around a second cleat with the same casual grace. The mariners on the barge waiting to load up didn't really notice. They've all been to Sasebo many times.

In the front and one side window was a paper sign that read, 'USNS Hudson.' That didn't matter on this end of the ride, but in port there might be other ships also using liberty boats to get ashore. If you get on the wrong liberty boat, for security reasons, they can't just drive you over to your ship. You must do the round trip again, plus the wait at the pier for the next liberty boat to leave. It could be a three-hour mistake. Pro tip: having eyes clear enough to read at the end of the night is important.

Once the deckhand secured the boat to the breasting barge he invited everyone onboard, "Daijōbu."

\* \* \*

This first night of liberty, I hung out with Teddy and Janice. Captain Brown said he might join us, but Teddy let us know that meant he was going to stay in his cabin and talk to his wife and kids for a while and then probably play Call of Duty all night. That was the captain's polite kiss off.

We climbed to the open seating on top. Nigel and Rachel were late arrivals and joined us for a breezy ride to shore.

I hadn't seen Nigel since the 'episode' in sick bay. First thing, he started to retell 'the story'. I can't even say the word again. I shrank into my seat and wished I could throw myself overboard. They were all taking great pleasure in my discomfort, laughing and carrying on.

I tried to defend myself, but Janice wasn't having it. Every time I started to talk, she made a loud sound, "AAAGGHH!". The laughter cycle would reignite. I hated being the butt of the joke, but I only pretend hated it, because my discomfort made it funnier for them. Hey, if you're going to lob bombs, you should expect some incoming fire.

The laughter abated. I thought a legendary follow up was in order. So, I asked Nigel, "Hey bud, where do assholes like you come from?"

It stopped everyone in their tracks. Somehow, I had managed to take the air out of an open aired deck on a moving liberty boat. Everybody froze, except Nigel.

Without missing a beat, he said, "I suppose I'm from the same place you are."

It was good to normalize with Nigel, well, as normal as things get after someone had witnessed your worst joke ever.

Nigel and I did the usual 'where are you from' and 'where have you been' line of questioning.

Turned out Nigel has a very interesting past. He was born to Persian parents who moved to London in 1977. Nigel was born there is 1978. His parents moved his family to Seattle when he was three and he's a die-hard Seahawks fan.

The two most interesting things about Nigel were – one, he and Captain Brown have been on four ships together and are close friends. When they met, John Brown was a third mate and Nigel was an AB. Two, Nigel is fluent in Farsi.

* * *

The liberty boat drops us at the USO Fleet Landing on Naval Base Sasebo. The pier is long enough to fit two liberty boats on either side. Tied to the pier, we wait for the crowd from the enclosed passenger area to disembark first and then we move. As we walk past the wheelhouse the pilot is already feet up, resting between runs. The deckhand extends a hand to help each of us across the slight gap between the boat and the pier. Each one of us thanked him in Japanese, "Arigato." This deckhand was a comedian, because he replied, "Don't touch my mustache." This was funny for two reasons – one, he didn't have a mustache, and two, don't touch my mustache is a phase Japanese people use to teach Americans the actual Japanese phrase for you're welcome, dōitashimashite.

At the taxi stand just outside of Fleet Landing, Teddy, Janice, and me hopped into a cab and Nigel and Rachel hopped into another. We were all heading to the same place through, Pub Gramophone.

The taxis in Japan are different than any in the world. These cabs are spotless. The driver is spotless as well, in a pressed collared shirt, drivers cap, and white gloves. The doors have mechanisms that open them automatically. If you need help with luggage or entering the vehicle, the driver will assist you happily. The one thing about Japanese culture is if you're going to do anything, it's worth doing well. The drivers weren't lesser than, like it seems some cab drivers are deemed around the world. They are professional drivers.

Pub Gramophone was a ten-minute cab ride, not far from the front gate of the base. The short cut through the park made it about a fifteen-minute walk, but walking would cut into our beer drinking time.

The bar began immediately inside the front door and made an 'L' shape about half the length of the place. In the back were areas for couches and coffee tables. We bellied up at the elbow of the 'L' with our back to the couches and facing the front. Behind the bar were a bevy of stickers from ships that have visited Sasebo. Where there weren't stickers, there were one-dollar bills with signatures of sailors who visited. My dollar was near the front of the bar written in sloppy Japanese and signed.

The draw of Pub Gramophone was the relaxed atmosphere and their extensive music collection that played just loud enough to hear, but not so loud that you couldn't hear conversations. It was my go-to drinking establishment when I was stationed in Sasebo twenty-five years ago.

As it was back then, Kimiko was still one of the bartenders. She was very popular with the sailors. Everyone on base knew Pub Gramophone and Kimiko. If I had better game back then, I would have tried to court her. I wasn't alone in those thoughts. Before I got up the courage, one of my fellow corpsmen at the clinic, asked her out and eventually married her. He still lives in Sasebo today.

Kimiko was busy with another customer when we walked in and didn't notice us. We bellied up at the corner of the 'L' and waited to be served. When Kimiko arrived, she recognized me immediately and started speaking Japanese to me.

"I'm sorry Kimiko, after all this time, I've forgotten most of what I knew. I just never speak it anymore."

She touched my forearm, "That's a shame, you were starting to get good."

I introduced her to our group and explained how I knew her and her husband. After a few pleasantries the drinking began.

Kimiko gave us a copy of the album list and told us the procedure to get a song into the rotation. We spent the first thirty minutes compiling the playlist for our evening.

We talked about everything and nothing all night long. Everyone but Teddy paced himself. He was half-lit before too long and headed for full blaze.

He called Kimiko over, "Kimiko, Kimiiiko. What's the jar with the snake in it?"

"That's Habushu or Hubu Sake."

"Why, why's there a fuckin' snake in your sake?"

She glanced at me, silently asking if I had any control over Teddy. I shrugged. I'd never seen him have more than two beers before. We were entering new Teddy territory.

"I wanna kiss the snake. Bring that damn jar down here. I wanna kiss the snake!"

Nigel put his hand on Teddy's shoulder, "Chief, there is no way she is going to let you kiss that snake. She might serve you a glass if you asked nicely."

"That's a drink? I thought they just had a snake in a jar for display. What the fuck sick kinda joke is that?"

Rachel tried to reason with him in her own soft way, "Teddy, you're acting like an ass, leave the poor girl alone."

"I am? I thought I was just actin' a quesion. You're the one's bein' mean. Can somebody stop pulling my chain and tell me; why there's a fuckin' snake in the jar?"

Kimiko chimed back in, "Teddy, the snake is an ancient Okinawan tradition. They believe the snake and the sake combination give you energy and aid with treating some ailments."

"Oh." Was all he said. The habu sake discussion ended as fast as it begun.

I made a mental note to keep an eye on Teddy for the rest of the night. Nothing good ever happens after the words 'I wanna kiss the snake.'

Rachel had seen enough, she said, "Hey guys, we're going to head back and we're going to take Teddy with us. You don't have to come, we've got him."

Teddy was about to say something when Nigel cut him off, "Come on Chief, if the shoe was on the other foot would you let me stay out and get even drunker?"

"Crap, you're hittin' me with logic. Me brain doesn't do logic right now. The logic store is closed."

"OK then, you agree that I am now your logic. Logic says it's time to head back the ship and sleep it off."

With Rachel on one side and Nigel the other they escorted Teddy out of the bar.

Janice and I just looked at each other and simultaneously mouthed, "What the hell?"

"Janice, are you done or do you want to follow them back to the ship?"

"Do you have any other places in mind?"

I smiled, "Do I ever. Not to brag, but I've paid for the mortgages in a few of these places. We can walk to the next bar in two minutes."

We said goodbye to Kimiko and walked around the corner to Shooters. It was a bar run by a retired Navy man and his Japanese wife. The atmosphere was a little more open and brighter here. Janice and I each ordered the house specialty – a cheeseburger and Chu-Hi.

Two Chu-Hi later, and we were ready to head back to the ship.

* * *

The Akasaki Fuel pier was ready to receive us after spending just one day at anchor. One smaller base tugboat came to retrieve their breasting barge, and two larger tugboats assisted us in the move. An hour after hauling up the anchor, we were pier side in the shadow of Atago Main Shrine. A mile of hilly peninsula was all that stood between us and the open sea.

Businesswise, being at the Akasaki pier made it simpler to load the AFFF. That mattered only to those involved in the AFFF loading. For the rest of the crew, it meant buses that ran frequently and a shorter ride to base. They stopped at the Akasaki pier and Fleet Landing. Every half hour one bus left the pier to Fleet Landing and vice versa. The crew loved it. The only thing that would have been better was a personal vehicle.

While we waited for the AFFF to arrive by ship from Yokosuka, Japan, it gave us the opportunity to dissect the decisions made by our handlers on shore. There was always, largely without all the facts, speculation by the crew. 'Why did this happen?' 'Was it for our benefit?' 'Was it to just screw with us?' 'Was it to show us who's really in charge?' 'What do they know?' 'Half of them haven't even spent time at sea.' These discussions did nothing to solve problems, but it is the way of every crew that ever went to sea. Which leads the old sea going adage: a happy sailor is a bitching sailor. And apparently, we were downright giddy.

The truth, as I see it, the expired AFFF probably would've worked just fine. The real reason we didn't go to sea, even for a few weeks on a wavier for expired AFFF was the people off our hull, were thinking about headlines, not hazard. Nobody wanted to sign off on the risk, so we waited. Because it's always safer to stall than to lead, says the man who never had to make those kinds of heavyweight decisions.

So, we waited in the holding pattern and enjoyed what Sasebo had to offer, the Ginza!

\* \* \*

The Ginza is the main shopping district in Sasebo that runs about straight eight blocks. It is open air, but covered with an arched roof about two stories up. No cars allowed under the roof, except where the roof passes over the cross streets. It sounds like a mall, but it's not. The buildings are all separate, built mostly before the roof was added. The first floor of each building had a shop or two, in every genre imaginable.

We of course gravitated towards the street food. Gyoza, yakisoba, yakitori, and manjū were on the menu. Manjū was my favorite because the bean curd was an acquired taste. It separated the tourist mariners from the real salts.

When Janice didn't have duty, she and I would make the rounds of the Ginza and then stop in at Pub Gramophone. We'd have a quick beer and say hello to Kimiko. Once, while Janice was in the bathroom Kimiko came around the bar and sat next to me.

"Jack, is that your daughter?"

"No, I would have told you she was my daughter if she was. Why do you ask?"

"This is the third time you've been in here this week. She's been with you every time and you two act like your father and daughter."

"Nope, just a shipmate I get along with."

"Well, don't do anything stupid to mess up your dynamic. It's sweet to see that kind of connection."

"Oh, no...no, no, no, no. For one, you're absolutely right about her being young enough to be my daughter and two, I don't own a good poker face. If I were to get stupid, as you say, my wife would know by the 2 hertz difference in my voice over the phone. That woman's a witch or seer or something. Not. Going. To. Happen."

Then I laughed, "Besides it came up awkwardly and out of context at dinner one time and her response was 'eww'. I think I'm safe from a reverse attraction as well."

"Good. Because you know me. I'll hunt you down faster than your wife will."

She pointed to herself and then to me, signaling she was watching me.

Janice came back and said, "You look puzzled."

"Yeah, Kimiko just gave me the 'don't hit on Janice' speech.

"Eww!"

The kid knew how to hurt. Ego shattered.

* * *

The following morning, I was working in sick bay and SU (Supply Utilityman) Steven Buckley came to visit me. He had no medical complaints but had heard that I was stationed in Sasebo before and wanted some pointers about traveling by train to Fokuoka and to tell me he was going to visit Marine World.

"I love aquariums. I'm still a yearly pass holder to the Georgia Aquarium. I just love seeing the dolphins and the whale sharks! That place blows me away. Have you ever been?"

"Yes, I have been to the Georgia Aquarium. I loved standing in front of the three-story viewing wall. The whale sharks swimming by are so majestic. The 400-pound yellowfin tuna looked like minnows swimming next to them."

"And the beluga whale exhibit. The whole place is so cool."

He was smiling ear to ear. "I have tomorrow off too. I'm staying at a hotel in Fukuoka and returning on Friday. I'll tell you all about Marine World when I get back."

"I'll be looking forward to your report!"

* * *

All the department heads are issued a cell phone in every port; in case an emergency arises. That evening while I was walking through Ginza with Teddy and Captain Brown, the captain's cell phone rang.

He listened intently and the mood across his face went from jovial to sad.

"Oh, no...How'd it happen?" He slowly shook his head no. "No, you don't need to call him, he's right here with me. I'll tell him."

He listened again for a minute in silence. "We'll be back onboard as soon as we can. Get good numbers and we'll call them from the ship when we get there."

Teddy and I were anxious to hear what had happened.

The captain closed his flip phone and took a second to gather himself.

"Steven Buckly was killed today. He was crossing a busy street and looked the wrong way before stepping out into traffic. Evidently the driver was only going 30 kilometers per hour, but his head hit the pavement. They think he died instantly."

* * *

There were no words to say. Shock hung over the ship like a fog. The AFFF was delivered. The crew went about its routine, but it felt hollow.

We talked about what a bright young kid Steven was. We hardly had time to know him, but what we saw, we liked. He worked hard, smiled often, and was happy to be at sea. Six months in the MSC was all it took for him to become one of us. A mariner, a shipmate.

Two days later we left Sasebo without our shipmate. We had nothing to do with recovering his remains or dealing with his death. The captain did call his parents. He later told us that was the hardest call he'd ever made.

As destructive as the sea can be, it heals too. The waves calm the soul. The wind fills your lungs. The sun warms your face.

Once you get relaxed and rejuvenated it will remind you that life is for the living, and if you don't keep your eye on the ball, the sea will quickly change its mood and have you join your deceased shipmate at the bottom of the ocean.

# Chapter 7—Philippine Sea

When leaving Sasebo, we rarely went north into the Sea of Japan. Sometimes we went east into the East China Sea, but mostly we went south to the Philippine Sea. If the Western Pacific was compared to Sasebo, the Philippine Sea would be the Pub Gramophone, we spent a lot of time there.

*  *  *

While reeling from the effects of Steven Buckley's death, we loaded another 200 pallets of cargo and topped off our fuel tanks.

Life at sea for us was delivering the goods.

VERTREPs were mostly done with larger ships that had flight decks and helos to do the heavy lifting. For smaller ships, like frigates, we UNREPed the cargo at stations 4 or 5. In other words, it went over on a span wire, similar to the fuel, just a little different. The pallets are transferred across the water in balanced pairs using a transfer head, or as a single pallet hanging from the center.

This is quite the ballet. Pallets and fork trucks moving about. Full pallets going over, nothing comes back, until the end, when they send all the emptied pallets back and the 'carefully' packaged garbage. Not only do we bring the groceries, but we also take away the trash when they're done with it. Organic matter can go in the sea, but everything else is taken back to port, with a 'you packed it in, you pack it out' mentality.

We were so busy with UNREPs that week we barely had time to think. It was just one after the other.

One day we had the ships queued three deep on each side. A ship would finish fueling and get cargo, and within an hour, the next ship had taken its place. The pace was frenetic, and the next paychecks were huge. I didn't hear a single complaint.

\* \* \*

During my monthly galley inspection, I noticed the crew's mess was looking a little messier than in previous inspections. That had been Steven Buckley's job, managing the crew's mess and keeping the fourth deck clean. The fourth deck wasn't up to standards either. The decks I could let slip but the crew's mess being dirty was a matter of crew health. I needed advice.

Before I wrote my report I spoke with the captain. The Chief Steward, Benjamin Cruz, was the officer in charge of the cooks and the SUs. This meant, ultimately, he supervised the mess decks issue. However, it wasn't his fault he was a man down.

I had also heard through the grape vine, that he felt responsible for Steven's death. Saying, he should have gone with his gut and disapproved his request for time off.

An already sensitive man wasn't going to take the criticism well. It wasn't unusual to lose people without replacement, but this time the reason sucked, and it left nerves exposed.

I asked the captain, "Knowing how Ben is, how do we approach this without sending him over the edge?"

"Doc, I can't let the crew get sick and I shouldn't tell him how to do his job." He stopped and pondered.

"Give him the report straight. Don't baby him, but don't throw him to the wolves either. I want to see how he handles this."

"But..."

"But nothing. Sometimes adversity is like a whetstone, and it sharpens the knife. Other times it's a boulder, and it just fucks the knife up. I want to see how he reacts. Offer your services to work out any emotional problems he may have with Steven's death, but do not baby him. If he can't handle the pressure, I want to find out sooner than later. Understood?"

I must have looked like I needed more convincing.

"Understood?"

"Aye, Aye, Captain."

I wasn't sure if I was about to sharpen a blade or watch it snap. I was betting on the latter.

I wrote up the galley inspection report and took it to the Chief Steward's office to have Ben sign it.

Overall, it was a good inspection report. The galley looked great, Chiefs Mess was outstanding, as was the Officers Mess. There was only the one little problem.

Ben took a few minutes to read over the report at his desk. I stood just to his left, saying nothing. His eyes scanned the page, but his face stayed blank.

He placed the report on his desk, "I'm not signing this."

"Ben, I understand you're short staffed. That doesn't mean the job doesn't get done."

"I'm not just short staffed you asshole. Everyone in this department is hurting. Steven was everybody's friend."

"I know. I'm not putting you on report or even saying your staff is doing a bad job. I'm simply stating facts."

"Facts as you see them."

"Listen, I know you're all hurting. I'm hurting too. He was a great guy. Do you want to have a sit down with your staff and do some group grief counseling or I can meet everybody one on one. Hell, I'll stay up all night crying and hugging it out with every last one of you. What I can't do is let there be an outbreak because of unsanitary conditions in the mess."

"That's a huge fuckin' leap. A dirty napkin holder to the whole crew dying of dysentery."

"That's not what I said. Standards are standards. I'm sorry for your loss." His defiance pissed me off just enough that I lost my cool.

"Clean the fuckin' Crews Mess." Then I picked up the report and slammed it back down on his desk, "and sign the fuckin' report."

He signed. I walked out.

Over the next few days, I'd see Ben in the passageways, and he'd give me a threatening stare. I would just smile back at him and give him a friendly "Hello." I guess Ben was forgetting the old Navy adage, 'never piss off the cooks, the pay clerk, or the guy who keeps your shot record.'

I didn't have to fear the cooks though because I did the galley inspections. Besides, they already loved me, I treated them like teammates not subordinates.

However, the cooks did have issues with Ben. They didn't trust him.

* * *

Now the Purser (aka pay clerk) was someone I didn't want to mess with. Her name was Tatiana Jones. She moved to the US in her early twenties and married the most American-sounding man she could find, Robert Jones. You'd think he was a mariner too, but no, he was an accountant, and by Tatiana's reports, a very good one.

That left people wondering; what was Tatiana doing at sea?

I talked to her at her office window all the time, as it was just around the corner from my office. She wasn't particularly sweet nor was she mean. She was metered. She had the slightest accent and after talking to her over time, it kind of disappeared.

She wasn't a loner, per se, but she did spend a lot of her time alone. After every evening meal she would put on her yoga pants and walk laps around the flight deck. How did I know? The deck department told me so. How did they know? Because instead of actually doing their overtime work, they would stand in the aft truck tunnel and watch her walk.

I couldn't let the mystery of how the beautiful Serbian ended up at sea go unsolved. Occasionally, she would invite me into her office, which was always locked because it contained the money safe.

I found out that she came into the MSC by chance. A friend of a friend knew someone who knew someone...you know...clear as mud how that worked. Anyway...she started as an SU and worked her way up to Purser. Her husband was super successful, but he worked all...the...time. They didn't have kids, badabing, badaboom, she's in the MSC and lovin' it. She says he travels to meet her all the time. It just works for them.

I suppose it was no different than me being at sea and my wife having a career at home. Why the double standard?

Mystery solved, but it was her story to tell.

* * *

The UNREPs complete, we headed back to Guam. In flyboy parlance, this was a touch-and-go. We docked at the Delta pier on a Monday evening. The deck department was going to load fuel and cargo the following morning, and we would be back at sea in less than 24 hours.

Nobody wanted to head into town on such a short turn around, but there was a secret party weapon, Beer-on-the-Pier.

I mentioned that the Pursers office was locked. The Beer-on-the-Pier cooler was double locked, and the only key was in the captain's possession at sea. In port, the key was in the possession of its curator, the party czar, Third Mate Scott Barlow. His position was so important that Janice volunteered to stand his watch while he set up the pier.

The beer cooler was only a part of the whole. A special pallet held the cooler, and three folding tables, a dozen chairs, and a folding canopy rounded out the party pack. When arriving to port, and it was appropriate, this was the first item to be handled by the deck department. Captain Brown ordered Teddy, who ordered Nigel, who ordered a couple of ABs to get the job done.

It had the feel of a NASCAR tailgate.

The deal was very similar to the Diego Garcia Yacht Club. You paid what you wanted. Everyone stuffed a $20 in the cash box. Occasionally, when the cash box was overflowing, the captain would authorize a commissary run and serve free hot dogs or hamburgers for the crew. It was the same as we could get on the ship, but it was on the pier. Pier food just tasted better.

This night was a good night—cathartic, even. It was the first chance we had to unwind since Sasebo. At least a quarter of the crew was there, even Ben. Captain Brown started off by quieting everyone.

"You guys performed above and beyond the call of duty. We all hurt, but we did our job. I've never been prouder of a crew than I am of you guys right now. I didn't know Steven Buckley well, but over the past week I've heard a lot about him. I'm sure he would have been one of my favorites. Tomorrow we're going to be busy as hell...again. And I know you'll show up and do your job. Tonight...Tonight, let's take some time to eulogize Steven Buckley."

He raised his beer, "To Steven Buckley."

Everyone raised their beers, "To Steven Buckley!"

The pier was somber, some were openly crying. Ben was crying the hardest.

The captain walked over to him and placed his arms around Ben's shoulders.

"Do you want to go first?"

"No...I'm so sorry...I didn't mean to..."

More shipmates surrounded Ben and hugged him, "It's not your fault."

One by one people spoke up and told stories about Steven. Some were heartfelt, some were funny. Every story was filled with love.

For ten days the crew grieved alone. This Monday evening in Guam the crew finally got to grieve together, with beers bought in ports all over the world.

I think Steven Buckley would have thought that was cool.

# Chapter 8—Viet Nam

A U.S. frigate off the coast of Viet Nam needed replenishment, not a usual location for us to perform UNREPs. But if there's water under our keel, we go where they tell us.

We're never privy to why active-duty ships are where they are. We don't fall into the need-to-know category. We yo-yo in and out of port so they can stay at sea for weeks or even months.

The scheduled rendezvous was six days away. The trip from Guam would take us seven days under normal circumstances. This means the engineers are going to don their spurs and kick a few extra horses out of the diesels.

Yeehaw. Buckle up. This ship is going to be rockin'!

During normal seas and normal operations, a ship the size of HUDSON doesn't move that much. A little pitching, a little rolling, just enough to rock you to sleep at night when you're nestled in your crib, err...bed.

At the, I can't tell you 'cause it's classified, speed of xx knots, the T-AOs like to shimmy a little. It's not drastic, but it's noticeable to those who have spent time onboard.

\* \* \*

A new AB checked onboard during our short stay in Guam. He was much older than the average AB, like my age. AB work is a young man's game.

The morning after we left port, the new AB, Roger, was waiting outside my sickbay door. One look and I knew he wasn't doing well.

He was using the bulkhead to support himself. His breathing was labored and shallow. When I touched his arm to help him into sickbay it was warm.

I helped him up to the exam table and took his vitals. 102°F temp and oxygen saturation, PO2, of 81%. Normal PO2 levels are over 95%; doctors consider levels below 92% as worrisome.

I listened to his chest. His heart was normal. Both lungs sounded like coffee percolators. Without the benefit of x-rays, because there isn't an x-ray machine onboard, I made the call of double lung pneumonia.

I admitted him to the ward. I started him on the appropriate IV antibiotics and oxygen.

When I notified the captain, his initial response was, "Are you kidding me?"

I assured him that I wasn't above joking around when appropriate, but I have never joked about double lung pneumonia before.

"Keep me in the loop."

I could hear the concern in his voice.

It was the weight of command.

An unusual mission and a sick mariner. How do you decide which mission is more important than a person's life?

It wasn't the captain's call alone. He'd have to report to higher ups and they'd have their input. But when it came right down to it. It was his ship, his mariner.

A luxury I never had on submarines, was the ability to call Telemed to back up my diagnosis and treatment plan.

MSC Medical in Norfolk, VA was also in contact with the higher echelons of MSC and told me to hold off on requesting a medevac for 24 hours.

Normally this was an easy call to make. This mariner needed a medevac. Whatever we didn't know about this mission must have been big. There was no use crying about it though. We were out in the middle of the ocean alone. We had no choice but to do what needed to be done.

It was time to reinforce my knowledge, hunt for that one bit of information that might save the mission and the patient.

All the medical books in my library treated the topic like the patient was an inpatient at the Mayo Clinic, because why in the world would someone with pneumonia be anywhere else?

Roger was about 8,000 miles from the Mayo Clinic and at least 400 miles from Guam. Soon we would be halfway between Guam and the Philippines.

No one off the ship was suggesting we turn around.

After reading a few more medical books, I switched to the Hospital Corpsman 3&2 Training Manual. It was my first study guide in the Navy, and damned if the answer wasn't right there in the baby doc book—chest percussions.

I was going to thump his back like a Rose Bowl half-time marching band drummer.

I took his PO2 again, 85%. The oxygen was helping, but not enough.

Roger balked at me percussing his back. I cupped my hands and gave a few blows to the front of his chest as an example of how it would feel.

"I guess that won't be too bad."

We carefully flipped him over, making sure his IV and oxygen hose didn't get tangled. I had him diagonal on the bed so his head hung over a lined garbage can and I started to percuss.

It took a few minutes before we saw results. But they came. He started coughing and producing tar black sputum. AND IT STUNK!

I excused myself and got a face mask and sprayed it with some peppermint oil, an old trick I learned from a diener.

Now that I wasn't about to vomit, my percussion efforts became effective again.

His PO2 after the percussion treatment was 89%. We weren't out of the woods yet. Everyone, most importantly Roger, was breathing just a little easier.

The decision was made. Roger stayed onboard unless his condition drastically worsened.

And you know what caused it all? Roger was a two-pack a day smoker for 40 years and four days before he came onboard, he quit smoking cold turkey. The little hairs that sweep particles out of your lungs (cilia) are paralyzed by smoking. When you stop smoking, they wake up and start to sweep at the stuck-on grossness out of your lungs. Ergo: All the stinky sputum his body was trying to expel was filled with tar and smoke.

He stayed the ward for four days. I percussed his back four times a day. His symptoms were up and down, but trending towards better. His total time on the ship was 10 days. He never worked a second.

\* \* \*

As a seasoned looky-loo mariner, there are some routes that you look forward to. Such is the case when you weave your way through the Philippine Island using the San Bernadino Straits.

The passages can be a little tight compared to the open ocean, but that's what makes it so beautiful.

The hills are a lush emerald green. The sky is almost always clear. The cities are few and far between. The shoreline looks like it's from a time long ago.

Mostly when we're near a port we're looking at massive shipyards and naval bases. Nature has been practically wrung from them.

Standing on the bridge I don't think the mates share my enthusiasm for our surroundings.

There is sea traffic everywhere, especially little fishing boats running perpendicular to the shipping lanes.

Shallow waters are never a captain's best friend. Nobody wants to end their career by accidently parking their ship on a coral reef.

We made it through the islands by the end of our third day out of Guam.

Roger was improving.

Captain Brown and the mates on the bridge were more relaxed.

Things were looking up.

\* \* \*

Mariners are a crafty bunch. Every mariner is a graduate of 'noticing school.' They observe everything, except if it's a part of the job they don't want to do.

Ubiquitous cell towers have only been around for twenty years. Anywhere along our normal routes, they have mapped out where those signals are.

For half a day on day four heading to Viet Nam, we passed as close as we could to the western part of Luzon, the northernmost island in the Philippines.

Our only UNREP was still two days away. The crew wasn't feeling much pressure. If we had deck chairs, they just might have been out on deck sunbathing. Practically everyone was outside on the starboard side, the side closest to land, looking for a cell signal.

The captain was lenient towards the behavior. He drew the line at working overtime after hanging on your phone half the day. The crew thought it was a fair trade.

Being international by nature, the mariners where phone-plan savvy. Many of the crew on the HUDSON were from the Philippines, or married to a Filipina, or just been in the area long enough to have Philippine SIM cards.

They had SIM cards from all the countries we traveled to most.

Me? I had a US based international phone plan, but because I was a department head and needed to make frequent call to the states for my job, I had a code to dial off the ship anytime I wanted.

I called Chloé daily. I told her I was only allowed ten minutes, so I'd get the daily download from home, and she would get to hear me say hello.

Therefore, when the cell signal was present, I wasn't trying to call anyone, I was looking for sports scores.

* * *

The Philippines faded from sight as we started the final leg to our destination off the Viet Nam coast. By the afternoon of day six, the engineers were finally able to throttle down the engines. Our ride smoothed and we awaited contact with our customer.

The time of our scheduled UNREP came and went. No sign of the friggin' frigate and no word from higher echelons as to the status of our customer.

At 2100 that evening we received a message from MSC in Guam. It basically said—never mind.

We may never know why our UNREP was cancelled unless it shows up in the news.

Here's praying for never knowing.

Our follow-on orders were to meet the MILLER to give them the frigate's cargo and then head to Subic Bay.

After racing the equivalent distance of North Carolina to San Diego it was a bit of a disappointment to not complete the mission.

But it always seems to even out. For every shit sandwich we're asked to eat, it's followed up with a beer.

And the beer we love most in the Philippines is San Miguel.

* * *

It was more befuddlement than anger about our race to the waters of Southeast Asia. A little collective head scratching and the crew easily shifted their focus to Subic Bay.

The VERTREP with the MILLER was just the formality that preceded our ultimate goal.

The deck crew was a little pissed. They had prepared the cargo for sending across the span wire. Now they were forced to shuffle the pallets so it made sense for them to go under a helo.

Nigel and Rachel were the king and queen of the deck department. They were fun to be around, but slack off for a minute and they were down your throat with both steel booted feet.

I caught them both sitting in the bosun office taking a break from breaking ABs. I don't know what they were talking about when I walked in, but they got really quiet.

"What's going on? Why'd you get quiet when I walked in?"

Rachel looked to Nigel and back to me, "No reason."

"Really that seemed deliberate. I know you two, what are you hiding?"

Nigel revealed his left hand, and it was wrapped in a towel.

"I didn't want to bother you."

He removed the towel and firmly planted in the back of his hand was splinter the size of a toothpick.

"Why didn't you want me to see that?"

"I'm busy. We're getting ready for tomorrow and I know you'll want to get all surgical with me."

It's then I noticed his multitool open and sitting on the desk.

"Were you trying to get that splinter out with your multitool pliers?"

"Yes, I do it all the time."

I grabbed his hand. He wasn't going to be successful. It was buried too deep.

"I'm sorry dude." I point out the door. "To my office. I'm going to get all 'surgical' on your ass."

Rachel couldn't resist, "The splinter is in his hand."

It only took a minute to get it out. A little Neosporin, a small bandage, and Nigel was ready to return to work.

"Hey, Doc. Do me a favor, put an ace wrap around my hand so it looks like you did major surgery."

"Why?"

"I just want to play a little joke on Rachel."

Why not, a little tomfoolery never hurt anyone.

I used an elastic bandage and a cravat from my EMAT training bag to make a sling for his arm. Then I escorted him back to the bosun office.

Rachel took one look at Nigel and rolled her eyes.

"You two are so full of shit."

I was willing to try to push through on the ruse, but Nigel caved.

"You're right. I was trying to fool you."

Proof that not every attempt at a good sea story is successful.

It was also a reminder that I wasn't there just for the big issues. Sometimes the minor things were just as important. And having a little fun along the way didn't hurt morale either.

* * *

Sometimes I went weeks, or even months, between medical issues that required more than handing out band-aids for boo-boos.

Some days I was just the guy with the supplies. Other days, I was an ear. The ship's mother. The priest. The therapist.

I didn't mind, that was the job.

The only thing I couldn't stand? Sympathy seekers. I gave it freely when needed, but if you came looking for it, I'd point you to the dictionary, right between shit and syphilis.

Still, when a soft heart was needed, I did my best to dig one out from beneath the layers of sarcasm and false bravado.

When Gina walked into my office, she got right to the point.

"Doc, I found a lump in my right breast. In the shower yesterday. Checked again this morning. I don't think I'm imagining it."

We talked for a few minutes. I took a proper history, kept my tone calm, and practiced being on my best behavior.

Then it was time for the exam.

"Gina, I need to get a female crew member to standby."

"That's not necessary. I trust you."

84

"I appreciate that. But it's procedure, and frankly, it makes me more comfortable, too."

"I'm not having one of those gossiping bitches in here while I get a breast exam. I said I trust you."

I gave her a tight, uncomfortable smile. "Still gotta follow protocol."

I turned to the phone to call for a standby.

"Doc."

I looked back.

In the blink of an eye, she'd moved from the chair to the exam table and stripped off her shirt and bra.

Sitting there, bare-breasted, she said, "I've breastfed four kids. More people have seen my titties than I care to count. Now shut up and do the exam."

My brain short-circuited. I tried to compute the possible outcomes of this situation and came up empty.

Gina snapped me out of it.

"Doc. They're just breasts. Get over here and help me. I need to know if I'm imagining this or not. I'm just another patient. Get out of your head and do your job."

She laid back on the exam table, placed her left arm behind her head, and added, "You start with the normal breast, right?"

She was right. That simple cue flipped the switch in my brain. I was the MSO again.

And yes, she did have a lump in her right breast. It could be nothing. It could be cancer. I didn't have that training or the equipment to make that determination. She'd be leaving the ship next port for evaluation and treatment.

She thanked me for helping her. But really, I should've been the one thanking her for her calm and how it helped me.

* * *

The next day we met the MILLER just hours outside the entrance of Subic Bay.

The undelivered cargo? About 40 pallets of assorted food and parts, and one special pallet: ice cream. The reason ice cream is special is two reasons. One, duh, its ice cream, and two, in the hot tropical sun, we must leave it in the freezer box right up 'til delivery time.

If it made sense to have a special fork truck with lights and sirens, we would. Every time there's ice cream in the cargo, the radio chatter is dominated by ice cream talk. I've seen a single pallet with $4 million worth of repair parts get delivered with less fanfare than ice cream.

I like to believe that someone a long time ago was fired for delivering ice cream soup. From that date forward, ice cream ruled the UNREP / VERTREP schedule.

For ease of navigation after the VERTREP, the MILLER chose a course going due north with us trailing in their starboard quarter. If the math was correct, the evolution would be complete in time for us to make our turn to Subic Bay.

The VERTREP with the MILLER was unremarkable. Two pro crews performing like pros.

The already palpable excitement reached fever pitch. The conversation turned to their favorite restaurant, bar, or beach.

When I got to the bridge the chatter had gotten so out of hand that the usually mellow Scott Barlow had to raise his voice.

"Mind your station! Quiet on the bridge."

What Barlow didn't know was that Captain Brown was entering the bridge just as he said it.

The captain found me over by the coffee mess and asked,

"Did he do that for my benefit?"

"No. He never saw you. He was getting pissed and they deserved it."

The captain nodded his head in approval, "Good on him. I was beginning to wonder if he had it in him."

"Oh, he does. That's not the first time I've witnessed it. Quiet doesn't mean weak."

"Are you telling me that because you think I don't know?"

"No, I'm telling you because I've only known you for three months. I'm not fully aware of your powers."

The captain looked amused, "Really? Like what powers?"

"Well, the powers of observation for one. I'm trying to unravel that one right now."

"Are you always a bit of smart ass?"

"Yes"

The captain laughed, "Cool, just not in front of the crew."

"Aye, Aye, Captain."

\* \* \*

The HUDSON made its way into the mouth of Subic Bay.

The wide entrance was flanked by low-lying hills. As we crept deeper into the harbor, the green gave way to the bones of old Navy life, bases long since turned over.

Cubi Point Navy Air Station was now Subic Bay International Airport.

The Old Naval Station had become the Freeport Zone.

And the shipyard? Now owned by Hanjin. Different flags, same rust.

We were heading pier-side at the Freeport. And across from us, maybe 100 yards away, stood the Liberty Bar.

The beer czar would be off this port. The Liberty Bar was just the beginning.

Beyond the gate, Subic spread out like a drunken buffet; bars, restaurants, karaoke joints, and tattoo parlors stacked elbow to elbow.

After a sprint to nowhere, a pneumonia scare, an overdone splinter surgery, and enough diesel fumes to choke a horse...we had earned a little madness.

This port is always fun.

Time to log off, lace up, and disappear into a different kind of sea.

The sea of humanity.

# Chapter 9—Subic Bay, Philippines

The anticipation for arrival in Subic Bay was different than other ports. For one, easily a quarter of the crew was of Filipino descent. The other reason? Most of the sea stories mariners swap in the Western Pacific seem to begin in Barrio Barretto—aka THE Barrio.

The cherry on top for this stay, it's Christmas time.

The first line hadn't even been tied to a cleat before mariners were stacked up on the tank deck, itching to hit the shore.

Young fools. The seasoned sailor knew better. The only people allowed to cross the gangway right after arrival were the local port officials, whose blessing we needed before anyone one could disembark the ship.

We'd just arrived from parts unknown. The local authorities had to give us clearance. At the arrival brief, we handed over paperwork confirming the crew was healthy and that we weren't smuggling anything sketchy. The parlance took time.

Roger was waiting with packed bags in sickbay. He was better, but far from cured. His breathing still wasn't normal. He was weak. My first order of business was to get him to the old naval hospital, now Allied Care Experts (ACE) Medical Center.

\* \* \*

What I had learned while arranging Roger's medevac was that he lived in Olongapo City, the city surrounding the Freeport Zone. Technically, once he set foot on the pier, he was considered detached from the ship and no longer my problem. I didn't think that was right, so I went to the hospital with him.

We arrived at the emergency room, and they immediately swept him away. I wasn't allowed to follow. About thirty minutes later, Roger's wife and two children arrived and joined me in the waiting room.

Soon the doctor came out to talk with us in the waiting room. Most Filipinos spoke English, but hers was perfect. I could tell she'd done her medical training in the States.

"Mrs. Dobbs?" She said gently.

"Your husband has double pneumonia. X-ray's show he has infiltrates in all five lobes of his lungs."

Mrs. Dobbs just nodded.

"He needs to be admitted. He's a very sick man, but he is refusing inpatient treatment. He could die without it."

She turned to me, "I'd like you to speak with him. He's your shipmate. Maybe he'll listen to you."

Sure, I beat the phlegm out of him a few days ago, but that didn't mean I really knew him. I owed it to Roger, and to this young doctor, to try.

Roger wasn't having it.

"Shit Doc, I was doing better at sea with just oral antibiotics. There's no way I'm going to stay in the meat locker of a hospital and die, when I could be at home with my family on Christmas."

"You're reading this all wrong. I've had a look around. This isn't Johns Hopkins but it looked fairly modern to me. You don't spend money on all this fancy equipment without having the people to use it. Your 'meat locker' assessment is way off."

"I live around here. I've heard things."

"It's your decision, but I think you're making the wrong one."

If I had known him longer, maybe I would've had more sway.

I let the doctor know he was still set on leaving.

She was disappointed, but thanked me, for taking care of him, and for trying.

The drama had gotten real, but I wasn't deeply connected to Roger. Despite the voices of my better angels, I walked away.

I have no idea how the Roger story ends.

Some stories just aren't ours to complete.

* * *

By the time I returned to the ship, it was duty crew only. I could've fired a shotgun randomly anywhere and most certainly missed everyone.

After a quick change, I went door-knocking on the fifth deck.

Nobody was home.

On the sixth deck, the captain's door was open. He was on the phone but waved me in to have a seat.

A minute later, he hung up.

"What are your plans tonight, Doc?"

"I don't have any. I was looking for a posse and then I was going to get something to eat."

"Have you ever been to Texas Joe's?"

"No."

"Then that's it. You and I are going."

In ports like Subic Bay the captain and chief engineer get cars with drivers.

Literally within minutes, the captain's driver, Freddie, had us standing in front of the neon-trimmed replica of the entrance to the Alamo, Texas Joe's.

We both ate our fill of ribeye and potatoes.

Unlike the food, the conversation was light.

"Captain..."

He cut me off immediately.

"If we're going to have a nice diner you need to cut that crap out. My name is John."

"Ok...John"

Even though we shared a first name, it felt different in my mouth when I said it loud to him.

The respect for captains, beaten into me from years in the navy, didn't evaporate easily.

Though there was a big difference now.

When I was in the navy, I was a young whippersnapper. A 25-year-old, calling a 50-year-old by his first name might seem weird. But now, I'm in my upper 50's and the captain is 48. Changes the dynamic.

The meal sated our appetite for food, but didn't come close to filling our needs.

We needed alcohol.

We climbed in the Freddie's car.

"How was your meal, gentlemen?"

John and I looked at each other. Was he talking to us? Gentlemen? He had to be. We were the only people in his car.

The captain responded, "The meal was awesome Freddie. Now we're going to need a roof top bar. Got any suggestions?"

"I know just the place."

Freddie drove us exactly eight buildings down the street.

"You're here. The Subic Park Hotel has a roof top bar with a view of the bay."

"Damn, Freddie. You work fast."

"Yes, sir. Will you be long?"

"I believe we will, Freddie. Is it time for your dinner break?"

"Yes, sir, it is."

John opened his wallet and offered Freddie a crisp $100 bill.

"We're going to be here for a few hours at least. Go pick up your wife or girlfriend and go back to Texas Joe's and stuff yourself like we just did."

"I can't take your money, sir. It's strictly forbidden."

"Oh bullshit, Freddie. Nobody in this car is going to say anything. Take the money."

I figured there was no such rule, Freddie was just playing it cool. Of course, he took the money, but I sincerely doubt he used it for steak. He probably spent $2 on pancit and pocketed the rest. We never asked.

* * *

The roof top bar was just what the doctor ordered.

We picked a table at the railing. The city was at our backs, and ahead of us: the green hills we passed on the way in, and the sea we were momentarily free from.

The banter stayed light, until the third round of beers.

John's expression shifted.

"Doc..."

I cut him off.

"If we're going to have a nice night out, you need to cut that crap out. My name is Jack."

"Touché, Jack."

"So..Jack...You took the Hippocratic oath, right?"

"No, that's for doctors."

"You took something similar, right?"

"Corpsman's Creed comes close."

"Right. My point is, whatever I tell you, you gotta keep it a secret."

"Now I think you're talking about a priest."

"Confess your sins to me, son."

He grimaced, "What I'm trying say here, you smart-ass son of a bitch, is that I need to vent, I need to know I can trust you."

"Yes, John. I will keep your secrets until I die, or unless I write a book. If I write a book, I'll change your name so nobody will know it's you. Sound fair?"

"Like you could write a book."

"You know, if you open the valve, I may have to bleed some pressure too."

"Deal."

The rest of the evening, the beer flowed. Then the shots.

His frustrations came out first, some I couldn't fully relate to, but I knew enough to empathize, to be an ear.

Others we shared. Distance from family. Kids growing up without us. Mortgages. Politics. Silence where connection used to be.

And he listened as much as he talked.

The longer we sat, the easier the beer went down, and the looser the words became.

Then came the mental guillotine. A sharp mood shift.

"Goddamn, Jack, we're s'pose to be celebrating. Let's go sing karaoke."

John called Freddie. We settled our sizable tab with a large tip and left the bar.

"Freddie. Do you know where we can get some Lambanóg?"

"Yes, sir."

We made a quick stop and returned to the ship.

Our state was not unnoticed by the gangway watch standers, including Janice, seated next to the folding table.

I walked over to her, placed my hand over her mouth, and kissed the back of my hand.

Her eyes grew wide, and she pushed me back by my shoulders.

I crowed far too loud, "Lucy, I'm home."

She laughed. If it had been anyone else, it would have been the end of my career.

John just shook his head.

In the elevator I hit the button for the fifth floor, thinking the night was over.

"Nope," John said, "I'm gonna show you the best roof top bar in the world."

John pressed six. We got off and walked up to the bridge.

I said, "This isn't a roof top bar."

"You, sir, are correct. But we're not done climbing"

It was open to the sky. The flying bridge was above the rest of the world. Just the wind and stars and two drunken sailors with a bottle of coconut moonshine.

The topic turned to music.

We passed the bottle of Lambanóg back and forth, singing our favorite songs into the night.

The universe smiled.

I think it was enjoying our concert.

* * *

The next morning, over breakfast in the officer's mess, Janice came up to me and said,

"Ricky, you've got some 'splaining to do!"

I smiled, even though my head was screaming, 'Kill me now.'

"What's the matter, Doc? Don't feel like ya did last night?"

I just looked down at my breakfast. I knew I should eat, but stomach was in full protest.

Janice wouldn't let it go.

" You know I sat on the bridge for two hours past my watch and listened to you two fools caterwaul at the moon?"

She was just going keep going until I said something, so I gave in.

"Did we sound that bad?"

"Some songs? Absolutely. Other songs...weren't too bad. You two actually have decent voices."

"Oh?"

"Do you remember kissing me on the gangway?"

"I wasn't that far gone. I kissed the back of my hand."

"Damn, I was hoping you didn't remember. I was going to get a lot of mileage out of that."

"Well, I do remember."

I looked down at the eggs and my stomach did another flip-flop.

"Is there a point to interrupting my breakfast, or are you just here to bust my balls?"

She laughed at me, "Nope. No business. All ball busting."

I didn't see the captain at all that day. I heard rumors he'd contacted the bridge for a few daily reports, but his cabin door never opened.

I wasn't much that day either. Tatiana saw me once in the passageway on the fifth deck,

"Heard you and the captain opened a karaoke club on the flying bridge"

I just nodded and quickly disappeared back into my stateroom without a word.

* * *

Back in the day, I could shake off a hard night like a champ. Nearing 60, the body takes a few days to forgive you.

By day two, I was feeling like a light meal and maybe a couple cold beers. The Liberty Bar was right there, I could see it from sickbay porthole. What harm would a burger and a couple drinks do?

As shipmates will do, I was given several rounds after I reached my preset limit.

"Hey Doc. Have a beer with us."

"Hey Doc. Do a shot with us."

"Hey Doc..."

I finally caught on after the sixth or seventh "Hey Doc". I'm quick on the uptake like that.

I stumbled the few yards back to the ship and hit the rack. It was only 2100, I figured a tight ten in the bunk and I'd be a new man by the morning.

At 0130, my stateroom phone rang.

"Hey Doc..."

At first, I thought it was one of the guys from the bar was pulling my chain.

"Missy isn't responding."

"What?"

"I was out drinking with Missy, and she just passed out."

"We're in port. And you probably drove her past the hospital to get her here. Why did you bring her onboard?"

"She's here Doc. Just come down and take a look. We're outside sickbay waiting for you."

Fuck, fuck, fuck, fuck. Every port brief, we explain where the hospitals are and what do in an emergency. Why don't people listen?

I threw on some sweatpants, T-shirt, and flip-flops.

The lights were harsh on my eyes. I squinted as I walked down the passageway. I wasn't buzzing anymore, but I was definitely under the influence.

Outside of medical, slumped against the bulkhead like a CPR mannequin, was Missy and her liberty buddy, Bill.

At least she was breathing. No obvious signs of CNS depression, thank God.

"Thanks for coming Doc"

I didn't give Bill the satisfaction of a polite nod.

"Help me get her onto the exam table."

He did all the lifting.

I called her name, no response.

Gently shook her shoulders, no response.

Applied mild pain stimulus using knuckle pressure on her sternum, still nothing.

Vitals: Stable.

"How much did she have to drink?"

"Six or seven beers and two shots of tequila"

"Did she hit her head?"

"No. Not that I saw."

I considered starting an IV but decided against it. I wasn't in good enough shape to trust himself.

I picked up the phone.

"Captain, Missy is down here passed out. I was out at the Liberty Bar for a while this evening. I think we could use some adult supervision."

While we waited, I finished the exam. No signs of trauma. No evidence of a bite or allergic reaction. It was just...too much booze.

The captain arrived. He was not happy.

I gave him the rundown. Bill confirmed the drinking.

"You were really thinking of starting an IV?" He asked, squinting at me.

"The thought crossed my mind. That's why I called you."

He took a long moment.

Here's what we're going to do," he said finally. Another pause.

"Bill, you're on drunk watch. Sleep in a chair in her stateroom. Leave her door open. Doc, you go back to bed and stay available. If she goes sideways, call the ambulance. Me? I'm going to bed and pretending this didn't happen."

We helped get Missy to her stateroom.

The next morning, I saw Missy in chow line like nothing happened. She was even cheerful when I said hello.

The captain wasn't. He stared at me the entire meal.

As I got up to leave, he spoke.

"I hope that's the last time you're that stupid. I'm really disappointed you didn't call me the moment you got to medical. If anything had happened, and it got out that you'd been drinking, we'd both be hung from the yardarm, just for fun."

"Got it."

"Yes, sir."

"Good."

I didn't argue. I didn't explain. He was right.

Another word about the incident was never spoken.

* * *

A week in Subic is like a month anywhere else. Everything is rush, rush, rush. We had three days left in port and the day before we left was a cargo load day. So today, Christmas Eve, was the last chance to do anything during the day.

Tatiana stopped by sickbay to see if I was available to accompany her to the Harbor Point Mall.

"What bus do you want to get on."

She looked at me with disgust, "Bus? It's only seven blocks away. We walk."

"Ok?"

"You know, you could walk more and lose a few pounds, you'd be more handsome."

"You're saying I'm handsome?"

99

"No, it's a relative term, you'd be more handsome. You'd go from a five to six. See, MORE handsome."

After being insulted, I wasn't going to go, but what the hell.

The walk took no time.

I had nothing to buy so I followed her around as she shopped.

We chatted about this and that, but nothing too deep.

After five or six stores. It was time for lunch. We stopped at a restaurant that overlooked the manmade drainage channel that flowed from the Santa Rita River. Back in the day, that it was called Shit River. It has been cleaned up since then, now apparently a 'worthy' backdrop for lunch.

After lunch, the bags just keep piling up. Ding, ding. I finally caught on. I wasn't her liberty buddy, I was her donkey.

Tatiana and I got back to the ship just in time to see Nigel, in a Santa hat, and Rachel walking off the ship.

Rachel addressed us.

"What are you two up to?"

"Just back from shopping at the mall."

"Cool, what to join us? We're heading to the Barrio for a pub crawl, starting at the Arizona."

Tatiana flatly declined. "The Barrio, that place is disgusting."

I was excited, "Give me ten minutes to shed the mall stink and I'll be right down."

Nigel wasn't having it. "Nope. We're moving. You catch up. We'll be at the Arizona for at least an hour. Any later than that and we'll be like smoke—poof—gone."

"Deal."

Tatiana waited until they were out of earshot, "Are you really going that dirty, stinky Barrio."

"Hell, yes I am."

I dropped her bags off at her room, changed fast, and hit the pier like a man chasing bad decisions.

* * *

The old Navy Base gates were still operational. Mariners had to show their ship IDs to get in, but I never understood what ID the Filipinos had to show.

Hey, I got on and off the Freeport. Guess it shouldn't concern me.

There was an ATM just before the gate. I stopped to pick up some financial reinforcement or as the sailors called it, peso-nality.

Barrio Barreto was a few miles northwest of the port and separated from the downtown area of Olongapo City by southward jutting finger of the Zambales Mountains.

Outside the gates were several forms of transportation waiting. The one I found the most fun was the tricycle, a 125CC motorcycle with a covered sidecar.

I agreed on a price for the ride into the Barrio and off we went.

As we climbed the long winding climb to the top of the hill, the trike lost piston compression. The bike was straining like hell but making no progress.

The driver was upset.

"No problem", I said.

I got out of the trike and started pushing.

Now he was confused.

We were about a 1/4 mile from the top when the piston failed, but the bike was light, and there were two of us.

In no time we crested the hill and the piston held without the uphill strain. We coasted to the bottom of the hill stopping at the first bar in the Barrio, the Arizona.

The driver, speaking in broken English, thanked me profusely for helping him push the bike up the hill.

I asked, "How much to fix the motor?"

He said, "3,000 pesos"—about $50.

I paid my fare and then tipped him 3,000 pesos.

"I'm sorry for breaking your tricycle. Merry Christmas."

"Merry Christmas." He thanked me again and drove off.

Inside the Arizona I found the love birds at the bar.

Everywhere else there were Filipina women, bar girls, trying to act sexy.

I said to Rachel, "I mean, I love the Barrio. It's a lot of fun. But why would you come with your man into this place with all the bar girls hanging around?"

Nigel shied away, which made me think Rachel was about to unload some dirt on Nigel. Instead, she revealed something about herself.

"These women do nothing for Nigel. This is for me. Watching them want him so bad, gets my motor running. V-room!"

"What, the mohawk not doing it for you anymore?"

She was in the mood to build up her husband's ego.

"No, the mohawk works all day, every day. I even have a sign on my stateroom door that says 'Caution: Slippery When Wet.' That's not up there because I just mopped."

Nigel didn't say a word. The grin his face just kept growing.

I couldn't handle it, "Rachel, that's too much information."

"Too bad. If that's going to upset you, we should probably part ways now. I'm just going to get nastier as the night goes on."

Rachel excused herself and went the restroom.

I leaned in to talk to Nigel over the music, "Holy shit, dude. My Aunt Shirley's a freak."

Nigel playful poked me in the chest, "Respect your aunt or I'll kick your ass."

"Seriously Nigel. I can tell. She's really in love with you."

"And I'm seriously in love with her. She's awesome."

"I can't wait for Chloé to meet her. They'll get along great, even though Chloé is nothing like her."

When Rachel returned, she announced it was time to hit the next club.

We turned left out of the parking lot and headed deeper into the circus.

* * *

Walking down the streets of the Barrio wasn't like the States. The buildings are close to the street and they invite you in.

The warm air seemed out of place with the Christmas lights adorning the buildings.

This area is known for its party atmosphere, but there were non-party businesses galore. The Barrio is alive 24 hours a day. We walked past many bars before the next stop, the Blue Diamond.

It was literally made from shipping containers. The upstairs bar was open to the street. We sat at the rail and people watched for one beer. Then it was time to move on.

Next up was The Hot Zone. This bar was the type of place that made the Barrio famous amongst sailors. The beer was cold, and the girls were barely dressed. We managed to find a table near the 'dance' floor. The unused dancer pole was candy-striped and labeled at the top: 'North Pole.'

Nigel and Rachel cozied up on one side and I slid into the other. A woman, who had to be 15 months pregnant, sat down next to me before I completely settled.

"Whatcha, drinkin'?"

Nigel ordered, "We'll have three San Miguels."

"Ok, I'll be right back."

For somebody that pregnant, she moved fast.

She placed the beers on the table in a group and sat back down next to me.

"You want to pay a bar fine?"

I hadn't even had a sip of my beer, and she was asking me if wanted to pay to take a girl home.

"No thank you."

Rachel and Nigel were raising eyebrows in judgement.

Rachel asked, "Well, Jack?"

"No! I'm a happily married man."

The waitress, also referred to as mama-san in these establishments weighed in.

"Your wife will never know. Look how young the girls are. So pretty. I promise you'll have fun."

"No, I won't"

Rachel just kept pretending to egg me on.

"Yeah, Jack. You'll have fun. She promises."

Nigel just sat quietly, making eyes every time the mama-san spoke.

"Are you a sailor?"

"Yes."

"Sailors always have a big appetite for girls. Why not you? Is your wife a beard?"

Rachel spit a little beer on the table.

"Yeah, Jack. Does your wife have a beard?"

Nigel corrected her, deadpan.

"No, she said his wife IS a beard."

"Oh, right, that make more sense."

The mama-san was relentless. Undoubtedly, she worked on commissions. After a few more minutes of harassment, I decided to stop playing defense and go on offense."

"OK, OK. I'll pay a bar fine."

"Which girl?"

"You."

"I'm the mama-san. No."

"That's the only way I'm going to pay a bar fine."

"You crazy."

"It'll help start your labor."

"I'm only seven months pregnant."

"Oh, I thought you were 15 months."

"That's not possible."

"Looks like you did it."

"You crazy."

Everyone had finished their beer. Nigel made the cut sign across his neck. We stood and walked out with the mama-san trailing us still telling me I was crazy.

As soon as we spilled into the street, we doubled over in laughter.

Rachel said, "What would have done if she said yes?"

"I would have paid her bar fine and then left without her."

\* \* \*

The end of the road for us was Whiskey Girl.

We stopped in there because the outside was painted with a US battleship firing broadside on one side of the door and dogs playing poker painted on the other.

No mariner could resist the dogs. It was too spot on.

The bar wasn't very big. The three of us took up a quarter of the seating. There were four girls who worked in front of the bar and a male bartender behind it. Compared to The Hot Zone, this place was tame.

The bartender served us each a San Miguel. One girl came over and sat next to me.

"What's your name?"

"Jack. Yours?"

"I'm Miranda."

"Nice to meet you, Miranda."

While Nigel and Rachel drank beer and acted lovey-dovey, I talked with Miranda.

I knew she was a bar girl, but she was polite, very pretty and easy to talk to.

We stayed at Whiskey Girl for four rounds. Miranda never asked me to pay a bar fine.

As we were paying our tab, I asked her about the bar fine.

"Miranda, you're a very nice girl, and I don't want to insult you. Are you a bar girl?"

"Yes. I thought that was obvious."

"I thought so, but you're not like the others."

"Yeah, those girls are taught to be pushy."

"How much is your bar fine?"

She told me.

I gave her three times her bar fine.

Nigel and Rachel were shocked.

"Merry Christmas. You're not leaving with me, but if you want to go do something else for a few days. You can."

She thanked me and walked us to the door.

"Are you sure you don't want me to come with you."

"Yes, I'm sure. Have a good evening."

We caught a Jeepney heading back toward the Freeport Zone.

Nigel and Rachel jumped out at the Arizona Beach Resort where they had a room for the night.

I got out at the gate and walked the mile back to the ship.

When I was younger, I might've taken her hand, paid the fee, and called it a good story. But Miranda was young. Too young. And I was someone's husband. Someone's father and a grandfather. I didn't need a moral epiphany, just needed to act like the man I told myself I was.

Besides, as Janice would say. "Eww."

# Chapter 10—Philippine Sea

The cooks are the most underappreciated, hardest-working mariners on the ship. While the rest of us staggered back aboard with bellies full of beer and street food, they were already back at it, cracking eggs, brewing coffee, and trying to pretend they didn't hear us rave about the restaurants ashore.

They're an up-before-dawn, work-past-sundown group of mariners.

Sure, they get breaks during the day, but it never truly ends. Morning, noon, and night the crew clamors for their hard-working bodies to be nourished. The cooks come through, every single day, even in port.

Their reward? A crew that constantly complains about the food. "It's not like my wife makes it." Or, "My grandma's is better." Or the highest of all culinary compliments, "It'll make a turd."

I tell you what, get your grandma to gather the stones to come to sea and cook for 90—120 complaining hooligans. Let's see how she does.

God bless the cooks.

\* \* \*

The chief cook, Ronald Morris, was from San Diego. We shared two passions related to our hometown, the Padres and the World-Famous San Diego Zoo.

During my daily walkthroughs of the galley, I'd always stop to see if he knew the scores from the night before. The Padres had just acquired some new players, so the excitement around the team was palpable.

Chloé was a huge fan and we were half-season ticket holders, forty-one home games a year. She had a work friend who was her baseball buddy in my absence.

She and Grace called their adventures at Petco Park "baseball capers."

Ronald and I would both be in San Diego during the maintenance period scheduled in Singapore next month. Chloé agreed that Ron and I should catch a game together. It's rare to see an MSC mariner when you're home, even in a Navy town like San Diego, you almost never see a shipmate ashore.

One day, we were talking about baseball nicknames and A-Rod came up. I suggested that his name lent itself to that kind of thing.

He said, "You gonna start calling me R-Mo?"

"No... I think your name needs to be flipped and then given the treatment."

He thought for a second, "Moron?"

"Close, Mo-Ron," I said, grinning. "It's not cool unless you give it that little bit of stank, **Mo**-Ron. Like you're more."

He rolled his eyes, but I caught him laughing later when someone else called him that.

Another silly nickname meant to be endearing, but was really just snark for my own amusement.

\* \* \*

Different people give you different nicknames. I've had too many to count. My Dad used to call me Pres, short for president, because my initials are JF and I was born in 1962 when JFK was in office. In college, I was just Son, short for Davidson.

But the most niche nickname I ever had was on account of my new position on the ship. Doc isn't really a nickname, that's more about people knowing your position and not your name. People transfer on and off the ship so routinely that if you didn't really get to know the person, there's about a zero percent chance you're going to remember their name even a month after they're gone.

Just like Doc, my new nickname came about because of a duty I was assigned.

With most UNREPs and VERTREPs, the last load to come across to our ship included a box of cookies, always freshly baked and usually chocolate chip. The box was quickly devoured by the UNREP crews.

Another hobby of those at sea is to collect memorabilia. Arrangements would be made to trade or purchase ship's ball caps, ship's coins, and other items.

One UNREP, the captain of the Japanese ship we were resupplying sent over a bottle of sake. Captain Brown was expecting it, but it disappeared. After that day, my official UNREP responsibility was to retrieve the cookie box and all its contents, report to the bridge with the unopened box, wait for the captain to inspect it, and then distribute the cookies and other swag as necessary.

It caused a lot of bellyaching at first. Deckhands howled like toddlers watching someone else open their Halloween candy, but eventually it settled into standard operating procedure.

The nickname—The Cookie Monster.

* * *

Of course, while I was busy defending desserts, the ship's long game was quietly shifting beneath us.

The schedule of a ship is always written in pencil at headquarters. Priorities change, ships break, shipyards don't complete tasks on time, and weather happens. Ships are aware of the penciled in schedule but usually don't start to make solid plans until a few weeks before. Operationally, it's a waste of time to plan too far ahead when everything changes anyway.

The crew on the other hand, despite an abundance of the evidence to the contrary, make plans like they're set in stone, especially if the schedule says the ship is going to the North Arabian Gulf (NAG), the preferred term of the US military, or, as the rest of the world calls it, the Persian Gulf.

Our current plans are to complete local operations in the Philippine Sea for the next few months, make our port visits in and out of Guam, and then report to Sembawang Shipyard in Singapore for 45 days upkeep starting in April. After the shipyard we would head to the NAG.

The HUDSON's good fortune when leaving Diego Garcia had turned around and bit them hard. Instead of a winter trip, we were now scheduled to be in the NAG in summer.

Nobody wants to be in the NAG in summer.

The relief requests came flying into the Purser's office.

You're required to give MSC Norfolk sixty-days' notice if you want to be relieved. It didn't always happen in exactly sixty-days, but it happened eventually.

The core crew was solid. My intentions were to take ship's funded leave, the MSC pays for my round-trip ticket home instead of flying in my relief and flying me home. Same cost to them. While the ship is in the shipyard for forty-five days with civilian hospitals all around, I'll go home and reintroduce myself into Chloé's life, again.

Chloé liked the idea and now I had a countdown to home. Sea time always seemed a little easier when there's a light at the end of the tunnel, as long as it wasn't THE light—"Hi, I'm St. Peter."

\* \* \*

Just like waves rolling onto the beach, the days at sea rolled one into the other. We'd pop into Apra Harbor for a day or two and head right back to sea. That's a high operational tempo.

When the cargo and fuel were low, back into port. Most visits we didn't even bother leaving the base. A quick trip to the commissary or NEX was all we had time for.

The captain's personal hero, and mine, was the beer czar. He was setting up and taking down beer-on-the-pier so often, he was beginning to think it was his primary duty.

Nigel would make it to the pier most nights too. I had started to become the third musketeer in their long-standing friendship.

One night, in my usual snarky banter, I said something that hit Nigel.

He didn't sound pissed, but he wasn't his usual self either.

"Do you always have to be a dick?"

It was so unexpected, I just stared at him.

When I finally found words, they weren't the right ones.

"That's no way to talk to your wife's nephew!"

"See that's what I mean. I was serious and you came back at me with a lame-ass joke. Fuck you, I'm out of here."

Nigel swallowed the last of his beer and headed back to the ship.

I turned to the captain, "What did I say that pissed him off so bad?"

"I don't think it's what you said, it was your tone." He paused, "You're a funny guy and you're fun to be around, but you didn't read the room. And unless someone is bleeding to death, you don't turn it off."

"Well, unless someone is bleeding to death, there's always room for humor. Besides, half my jokes are self-deprecating. And if he can't laugh at himself or his situations, then I feel it's my job to teach him how."

The captain disagreed, "See Jack, it's that attitude that gets you called a dick by the likes of Nigel. This OpTempo is wearing on him and Rachel. They're stressed. They're fighting. And you just shit all over his feelings, not intentionally, but you did it none the less."

"We're mariners, we don't have feelings, remember?"

Captain Brown shook his head in disapproval. "You just did it again. There isn't a joke that will salvage this situation."

I knew what to do, but I didn't want to hear it, "What should I do?"

"He's not one to hold a grudge, just say you're sorry the next time you see him."

The next morning in the chow line I stood next to Nigel.

"Sorry, man."

"Don't worry about it. We're good."

\* \* \*

There are ships and then there are aircraft carriers. We hadn't seen an aircraft carrier since I've been aboard the HUDSON. And even though I've been alongside aircraft carriers before, it's still impressive.

Today we are servicing the USS George Washington, CVN-73, homeported in Yokosuka, Japan. A city at sea. It is home to about 5,000 sailors and marines and it holds about 90 aircraft and helicopters.

Since a city of 5,000 consumes a lot of everything, sometimes it takes two supply ships to service it. We'll be supplying fuel only and the MILLER will be providing all the food and such via a VERTREP sailing on the opposite side of the carrier.

The ocean wanted to show off this day.

As the WASHINGTON approached from our port quarter, a massive pod of dolphins frolicked near the carrier. They were everywhere. A dolphin show at an aquarium never saw a show like this.

They were playing in the bow wake, they jumped high and spun landing tail first, they did forward flips and backflips. They were amazing.

We were still waiting for the WASHINGTON to get into position, so everyone had the phones out filming it. I overheard someone say,

"Steven Buckley would have loved this!"

\* \* \*

We could see the MILLER through the open doors of the hangar deck of the WASHINGTON. Two Pumas and a CH-60 were in on the action. It was non-stop motion on the flight deck of the carrier.

For our part, fuel hoses were going over at Stations 2, 6, and 8. The fuel crossed the gap between the ships with enough speed to fill up an Olympic-sized swimming pool every few minutes.

As UNREPs go this one was boring right up until it wasn't.

Aircraft carriers usually wait until they are over the horizon to start flight operations. This day something was amiss. The MILLER had completed their VERTREP and we were about 95% done fueling, when, without explanation, the carrier called for an emergency breakaway.

There was nothing but confusion on our side, we didn't see a cause, but the rules were, if you needed an emergency breakaway either ship could call it no questions asked.

We retrieved our fuel hoses as fast as we could and the carrier moved only about half mile from us before they started launching aircraft. Four F/A-18 launched in minutes.

The carrier went about its business and disappeared over the horizon. We went about the business of readying our decks.

About 30 minutes after the emergency breakaway, a jet approached us from our port bow, and flew down our port side at about 300 ft. A sonic boom shook the ship. Less than 5 seconds later, two F/A-18s followed the same track. BOOM! BOOM!

We never heard a word about the incident. I bet the Pentagon did.

* * *

There's an old navy saying that the two most dangerous things in the world are an Ensign saying, "In my experience," and a Navy Chief saying, "Watch this shit."

Nigel never made a show of it, but he had his ways—subtle, surgical.

Case in point: One morning, the Bosun found an abandoned paint bucket full of primer and a bulkhead chipped to bare metal where an Ordinary Seaman was supposed to be working. He painted part of the metal for the OS, but he painted just enough to spell out: "I'm watching." The captain and I walked by as he was finishing his artwork.

Captain said, "Who's that for?"

"OS Smith"

"Figures"

OS Smith was a bit of a sea lawyer. After a year in the MSC he thought he knew two things, his rights and how to 'skate' right up to the line, but not cross it.

Everyone was sick of dealing with his attitude.

One day we caught a break.

He reported to medical with two abscesses on his gums.

Normally, that's manageable, antibiotics, and wait until we hit port for dental. But two abscesses?

115

That's pushing it. Still not an emergency...unless the sailor in question is a complete shit-bird.

If I liked the kid, I would've helped him out. Maybe treatment in Guam while we went to sea and let him catch up after treatment.

But that wasn't the case.

I made my pitch for medevac, citing our OpTempo and the complications of keeping him aboard. MSC medical signed off. The captain and bosun were happy. Now I just had to tell the OS to pack his bags.

The strapping young man, six feet tall and built like a linebacker, came into my office.

"Doc, you wanted to see me?"

"Yeah. Your dental issues have earned you a medevac."

He scowled, "No, I refuse the medevac."

"Not your call. It's mine. Go pack your bags. Tomorrow's VERTREP you're transferring to the BRASHEAR and they'll take you into Sasebo, and from there you'll fly home. Once your root canals are complete and you're medically cleared, you can return to duty."

He puffed his chest and slammed his fist on my desk.

"No! I got responsibilities. I need the overtime."

He scared me. If this turned physical, I was going to lose. My Tae Kwon Do lessons from ten years ago weren't going to save me.

I decided that, like with a brown bear, or is it a black bear, you need to stand up for yourself and he'll back down.

Crap, I'm going to get mauled.

I stepped forward on what I hoped weren't obviously wobbly knees.

"This is my office and if anyone is going to slam their fist on shit, it's going to be me!"

It worked. He backed down.

He softened slightly and tried a new angle.

"Is there someone at MSC medical I can call to plead my case?"

Poor sap. Should've never backed down. Now the emboldened shark was going to eat the bear, brown or black, didn't matter.

"No, there isn't anyone you can call. We are at sea. And out here, medically speaking, I am the Alpha and the Omega. Case closed."

He didn't say a word.

I lowered my voice. "Now go pack your bags. You're on a helo tomorrow."

He left.

I sat at my desk, said a pray of thanks, and then laughed at myself. Who says shit like that?

\* \* \*

For all the drama on the decks and elsewhere aboard, there was always one daily respite, lunch in the Officers Mess.

At the head table sat, the captain sat at one end. To his left and right were the chief mate and me. The chief engineer held the other end, flanked by the first engineer and the supply officer. In the middle seats, opposite each other, sat the purser and the comms officer. All the department heads. All the usual suspects.

We'd talk casually about work, port gossip, the occasional gripe. But once the forks were down, the junior officers had left the mess, and the chairs scooted back to relax, Teddy took over.

He was larger than life.

At lunch? He was a theatrical release; directed, produced, and starring himself.

We came to call it The Teddy Matinee.

For the next 15 to 20-minutes, he'd give us a tight impromptu sit-down comedy set.

"It's only fair to tell you, my wife says that if you laugh it will only encourage me."

"I just got a new Apple Watch. Yeah, I'm an Applephile. Not a pedophile—an Applephile. I like little gadgets."

We'd roar. And like his wife said, it only encouraged him.

"Before I joined MSC, my mom thought I should be a comedian or a mortician. I finally decided to give her suggestion a whirl. Anybody want to be embalmed...No?"

"Hey Doc, I was bitten by a wolf!"

"Where?"

"No, regular."

We always knew he was wrapping up, because he'd close with the same line.

"I hope you had fun here today. Don't forget to tip your SU."

That one only works if you were MSC. The SUs were our mess attendants.

I guess it loses something when I have to explain it.

Maybe he wasn't funny at all to the outside world.

In our world?

He killed.

* * *

We pulled into Guam one last time, just enough fuel left to justify the stop, just enough weariness on the crew's faces to make it welcome. Nobody said it, but we were all counting down.

A few quick runs to the NEX. A few last pier beers. Nigel and Rachel were silent that night, sitting closer than usual. Even the beer czar was too tired to be smug.

We topped off tanks, stacked pallets, and tidied the ship. It felt like hitting replay on a song you liked six plays ago. Necessary, but no longer fun.

Then finally, we were headed to Singapore.

\* \* \*

Pulling into Sembawang always had a weird energy. The mission changed the moment we entered the Johor Strait. The pace dropped. The posture shifted. We went from sailors underway to maintenance workers in coveralls, fixing a ship that no longer needed us to run full speed.

Within hours, contractors were swarming the decks like ants. Equipment shut down. Work lists unrolled. You could almost hear the ship exhale.

I locked up sickbay, turned over the narcotics to the captain, and got to Changi for my flight home. Chloé was already texting grocery lists.

Forty-five days. No UNREPs. No Cookie Monster duty. No playing doctor for mariners. Off the ship, I wasn't licensed to do anything medical.

Just the quiet hum of a condo, the hustle and bustle of Little Italy, and a woman I hadn't seen since this all began.

I was going home.

# Chapter 11—San Diego, CA

I say a lot of nice things about the MSC. Their travel agency services are not something I'm going to rave about. They would route me through New Zealand and three cities in South America if it saved the government a penny. Fortunately, the finances of flying don't quite work out that way, but they do sometimes make for some weird itineraries.

The flight home took me from Singapore to Manila to Tokyo to Seattle to San Diego. I don't know for sure, but I think one of the agreements the government has with the airlines is they will give the government discounts on flights that are underfilled. And since so many government-paid flights are last minute travel, the airlines push the itineraries. At least, that's what I'd do if I ran the airlines. Still, after months at sea, even a chain of grimy airports feels like a breadcrumb trail back to sanctuary.

Flying into San Diego almost always brings you in from the east over the Laguna Mountains, buzzing the top floors of the taller buildings in Park West and Little Italy, and then onto the single runway at San Diego International Airport, aka Lindbergh Field.

With only one runway, Lindbergh Field operates like a finely tuned machine. As one plane lands, the next plane in line hurries out onto the runway, takes off, and not a minute later, another one lands. It's an amazingly choreographed dance.

\* \* \*

Chloé was waiting for me as I walked into baggage claim. We were excited to see each other, and if we had younger joints and stronger backs, she might have jumped in my arms, and I would have twirled her around. Instead, being the mature adults we are, I kissed her gently but quickly like I'd just returned from a trip to the grocery store. When you're in your upper 50s that's real love baby. No stints in traction required.

The drive to our condo in Little Italy is only ten minutes. The longest part of the whole trip is waiting for the left-turn arrow at Harbor Drive and Grape Street.

Chloé is a woman of convenience, and she doesn't like to drive, so Little Italy makes perfect sense for us. Almost everything she needs is within a five-block walk; markets, shops, and restaurants. For me, Karl Strauss, Stone, and Ballast Point all have tasting rooms equidistant from our building.

We had four weeks, and I promised myself I'd spend them figuring out how to be home again. She had developed routines that don't include me, out of necessity. I've built habits that only make sense at sea. And now, we had four weeks to pretend those worlds could overlap.

The first days at home are always the easiest. It's like getting married all over again, that's why it's called the honeymoon phase. She laughs at all my jokes. I don't mind all the subtle corrections that bring me back into her calm world. Then my snark gets to be too much, because I don't know how to shut it down. She tries to be accepting and understanding, but just how much fingernails-on-the-chalkboard behavior can one person reasonably endure?

It eventually leads to the first snap. She says something just a little too nit-picky for my tastes and I follow with full Chief-to-screwed-up-subordinate salvo. Then silence. We sleep back-to-back. No words in the morning. She goes to work, and I call my mom to complain.

How come I always assume my mom is going to be on my side, even when I'm wrong.

Nope, my mom is a double-barreled shotgun of truth to the face. Not very gentle, but highly effective.

"Jack, you cannot treat Chloé like a sailor. I talk to her all the time while you're gone and that is always her biggest fear when you return. You have to flip the switch. Be her husband, don't be Doc. Haven't you told me you're not licensed to do anything medical off the ship? Well, you're not licensed to be an ass off the ship either."

I had no defense. The only word I could muster was, "OK."

"Now be ready when she gets home from work. Go buy some flowers and take her out to a nice dinner. You owe her that. And most importantly tell her you love her and that you're sorry."

I thought for a second, "I'll do just that mom. I'm a flippin' grandfather, I already know that. Why do I have to hear it from you?"

"Because no matter how old you are, you're still a man who has spent too much time at sea. Why don't you stop this silliness and stay at home with your wife?

Then you won't have to go through an adjustment period two or three times a year. I don't get it."

I was practicing what she just asked me to do, so I swallowed the sharp retort.

"Thanks for your advice, Mom. I'll consider it. I think Chloé's sick of it too, but now is not the time."

"Love you, you pigheaded sailor."

"Love you too Mom."

* * *

I got flowers just around the corner from our condo at The Market by Buon Appetito and displayed them in a vase on the dining table. Chloé was always dressed to the nines for work, so I matched her with slacks, dress shoes, and a shirt she bought me for just such dining occasions.

When she arrived home, I said all the right things. She adored the arrangement I picked. She just wanted a minute to refresh her makeup, and we strolled at her pace for four blocks to Civico 1845. Along the way we passed through the Piazza della Famiglia. The old-world charm of people sitting outdoors enjoying the community and the view of the bay added to our elevated mood.

We adored Civico 1845 because the owner, Stephano, was from Naples, Italy. He lived in the next parco (neighborhood) over from us on Via San Nullo when we were stationed in Italy. Now we lived just blocks apart 20 years later. It's such a small world.

Stephano greeted us when we arrived.

"Ciao bella. Buonosera bello. Your table will be ready in 10 minutes or so. I assumed you'd like an

Aperol Spritz while you waited. You two are creatures of habit."

"Good call Stephano. We'll take those out to the Piazza. We'll be back by then."

Piazza Basilone is just outside their front door on the corner of India Street and W. Fir Street and pays tribute to Italian American Marine Corps Gunnery Sergeant John Basilone, Medal of Honor recipient for his actions at the Battle for Henderson Field in Guadalcanal during World War II. It's a solemn place to sit and reflect. Chloé and I did just that. We toasted to being together and then toasted Gunny Basilone.

Families with young children and groups of young adults unaware of what they were passing through, laughed and carried on as vacationers do. It didn't bother us. For their education, it would have been nice to take a minute of their time to notice who this beautiful piazza was honoring.

Our Aperol Spritzes consumed, we went back into the restaurant. A young lady who has served us several times before seats us and takes our orders.

The beauty of Civico 1845 is that it is authentic Italian food. The beer is Italian, and the cheese comes only from there. The kitchen staff speaks in Italian, and even some of the wait staff. I always butcher their language, but they are happy to let me try. Chloé lived in Italy too, but she's a bit of a Francophile from her days in school, so she sticks to English rather than risk insulting the staff by speaking French instead.

The setting was bellissimo, the food was fantastico, the beer was fredda (cold), and I can fit both my feet in my mouth at the same time.

The tensions of the night before were in the past; we'd moved on to have a nice dinner. We talked quietly about friends, family, and a few harmless work gripes, but nothing that stirred the pot. Unfortunately, there was a TV over the bar, and my side of the table was a prime viewing location. Chloé was telling me a story about something at work and...I interrupted her mid-sentence.

"Triple play! The Padres just got a triple play!"

Chloé, understanding I have a roving eye for sports, shook it off like a champ.

"Can we get back to our date now?"

"We're on a date? I just thought we were eating dinner."

She just stared at me, somewhere between amused and annoyed.

"Nobody thinks you're funny, and nobody thinks you're cute."

"Everybody thinks I'm funny," I said, smiling. "And everybody thinks I'm cute."

She didn't laugh.

That's when I knew I'd gone too far.

\* \* \*

Some of you may have asked, why didn't Chloé take off time when I first got home? It's simple, we don't always know when I'll be traveling so she can't always arrange to have days off. Thankfully Chloé has a cool boss, and I get along with him well. Cam understands our situation with my travel and has told me in the past he'd be as flexible as possible with time off.

Big screwups need big apologies. We had plans for a nice dinner for her 50th birthday and the end of the week, but given our last dinner out, I needed to go bigger.

I called Chloe's boss and arranged for her to have a week off and he promised to keep it a secret.

I had already arranged to take her to lunch, so I had the perfect excuse to meet her at 1100.

"Where are you taking me for lunch?"

"It's a surprise."

"Tell me."

"Not now. I'll tell you in about 20 minutes."

We drove past our condo, and parked in long term parking at the airport. I opened the trunk and took out two suitcases.

Chloé was starting to get pissed.

"We don't have time for this. I have exactly 40 minutes to get back to work."

"You have a week to get back to work, I arranged it with Cam."

"I can't go anywhere. I have work to do. Plus, you haven't the foggiest idea how to pack for me. Hell, I don't even know what I need. How did you pack for me?"

"Don't worry about the packing. Whatever I forgot, or you hate, we'll buy new."

"Ok, Jack. No more games. What the hell is going on here."

"It's your birthday on Friday, so I thought we could have your 50th birthday celebration in the 50th state."

She looked puzzled. "You're taking me to Alaska for my birthday?"

"No silly, Hawai'i is the 50th state. I'm taking you to Hawai'i."

"This isn't an elaborate joke, is it?"

I showed her our boarding passes.

She hugged me tight. "And I get to buy whatever you've forgotten, and I don't like. You might as well leave that suitcase in the trunk. We're shopping in Hawai'i!"

We always travel well together, and this time was no different. We ate well. We saw the sights in every corner of Oahu. And she shopped far less than I thought she would.

We came back rested, reset, and love renewed.

\* \* \*

A new honeymoon period had arrived, the second in two weeks. Chloé returned to work, and I spent time with projects around the house, walking the Embarcadero, and took in a few Padres games. Mo-Ron and I never hooked up for a game. He was busy with his family and besides, we saw enough of each other at sea.

I was set to fly back to Singapore that coming Monday. On the Friday before I left Chloé and I invited our good friends and neighbors, Jake Hernandez and Louise Jones, over for dinner.

There was a time between the Navy and the MSC I thought I could be an accountant. Jake and I met at San Diego State University. I was the old guy in every class, and he was about 10 years older than the average student, so we stuck out and stuck together.

I had just moved back to San Diego then and was going on about the first churro I'd ever had at the San Diego Zoo.

"Dude, those churros suck. The best churros are in Old Town. I'll take you sometime."

I know race, but I don't often think in racial terms. I knew both of Jake's parents were born in Mexico, but I never thought much about it. It was just a fact, not an issue.

Just then the professor called for everyone's attention.

"We're going to celebrate this month's birthdays on Thursday. Would someone volunteer to bring donuts?"

Because of the conversation Jake and I just had, I volunteered Jake, "Jake, says he knows where the best churros are. He'll volunteer to bring churros."

Everyone except Jake and I clutched their pearls. "You can't say that. That's racist."

Jake laughed at me, and I was embarrassed. Event over.

Two or three weeks later Jake invited me to his sister's house for a family event. When I arrived, he introduced me to his family,

"This is the racist friend I was telling you about, Jack, and his wife, Chloé."

I just leaned over and whispered to Jake, "Game on motherfucker."

For years when it was just us two, I'd say something that would be wildly inappropriate to him, but never in mixed company. He'd lean into it, call me a racist bastard, and the banter went back and forth reliving that one moment when the world misunderstood. It was our inside joke. Chloé and Louise knew about it as well, but weren't nearly as excited about it as Jake and I were.

Chloé took half a day off and cooked like she was trying to impress, even though our friendship was well established. The menu included salad, beef tenderloin, the most time intensive Hasselback potatoes, three different vegetables, and two pies.

And we feasted.

Later the conversation turned to work. Jake was talking about his accounting job and having an accounting degree myself I was able to hold my own in the conversation.

"You know Jack, you're lucky your temperament didn't fit with accounting, otherwise you'd be stuck in an office like me all day and not globetrotting, and not leaving your lovely wife behind."

An innocuous statement, but it hit me wrong. I decided the racist gag needed a return.

"Yeah, you're right. I'm lucky in two aspects. I'm not a working accountant and I don't have to worry about getting deported."

Chloé and Louise stopped their conversation and witnessed with mouths agape.

Jake shot back, "Hey asshole, I worry about getting deported all the time. I've never lived anywhere but in Southern California and I still worry about it."

"I know, you've told me before. I'm sorry."

Jake nodded to accept my apology, but he wasn't finished.

"Jack, you don't seem to know when the joke is over. The whole racist thing was funny for a while. That was ten years ago. We see each other all the time. I know our friendship is deeper than a stupid, ten-year-old joke about me having Mexican parents. It's not fucking funny anymore."

I hung my head low, "I know. It's just the way we act all the time at sea. I don't turn it off easily. I'm sorry."

"That's a crap apology, but I think it's the best you've got. Apology accepted."

The evening settled. The moment was gone. I felt bad and didn't make any more stupid jokes.

Jake was true to his word and acted like it never happened. A warning shot across my bow. Message received.

Later as we said our goodbyes, I gave Jake a bro hug at the door and said, "Hey, I'm really sorry about earlier."

"I know you are."

"I'll stop. I love you like a brother."

Jake smiled, "Yeah, I know you do."

"What? No love back for me?"

"No, you're too white for me."

"Touché."

Louise gave me a hug as well. "He really looks forward to our times together. So do I. Don't fuck this up with your stupid jokes."

"I never said I was sorry to you. Will you accept my apology?"

She thought for second, "Of course I do dummy, but you can go too far."

They left but that wasn't the end of it.

I had embarrassed Chloé.

The weekend was not as affectionate as I had hoped.

When I left on Monday, our goodbyes were flat. I was glad to escape further judgement. I think Chloé welcomed the silence more than the goodbye.

# Chapter 12—Indian Ocean

The captain and the chief engineer are the only two positions on the ship that are permanent positions. They still need breaks from the sea to be fully functional human beings. When the time comes, relief captains and engineers temporarily relieve them for two or three months.

While I was at home recharging myself, Captain Brown was relieved by Captain David Stetson.

Relief captains usually come in two types. Those with calm experience and those climbers who are trying to make a name for themselves. Their goal more than anything is to be noticed by MSC headquarters to get their own permanent assignment as captain. The irony is those who seek the attention rarely get it or get the wrong type of attention.

Captain Stetson showed his colors immediately. He was a toe the party line no matter what kind of leader. And the biggest hot button on the ships was facial hair. It was one of the traditions that separated the MSC from the Navy. Evidently it was the first words out of his mouth when walking onboard. He chewed out the gangway watch for facial hair before he had officially turned over with Captain Brown. That one move sealed his fate with the crew. I heard all about it before I ever laid eyes on the man.

We only spent a few days in Singapore once I was back on the ship. When I finally had a sit down with the new captain, we were already a day at sea.

He asked me into his office, and I sat down across the desk from him. Any traces of Captain Brown were gone. His appearance was inspection ready for the US Naval Academy. His tone was formal.

My appearance was pure MSC. Full beard.

"Nice to meet you, Captain Stetson."

No nicety. Just business.

"Why aren't you shaven? I assume you've heard the new policy that Captain Brown wasn't enforcing. I'm sure the crew has informed you of my enforcement of the policy. As one of my officers, you need to set the example. You need to be behind the shaving policy and enforce it 100%."

The stories I heard were not exaggerated. If this was who I was going to deal with I wasn't going to give him any quarter. I was going to be an official pain in his ass from the get-go.

"Captain, you are 100% wrong."

That should piss him off. Bet he's never heard those words ever.

"That's the new policy and I expect you to enforce as it is written."

"It's a bullshit policy written by an Admiral who has no clue what happens on the deck plates. The new Admiral hates civilian mariners and wants us to resemble active duty personnel."

"I don't think I like your tone, MSO."

"I don't like change for the sake of change. I don't like people pissing down my leg, telling me it's raining."

"There is absolutely no need for vulgarity in this office. Apologize."

133

"Captain, I am your MSO, this is your ship. I will be enforcing the MSC policy and your interpretation of that policy. That is my job. This is your ship. But...as your medical expert, behind closed doors, I AM going to tell you what I think concerning medical matters."

"How is beards a medical matter?"

"The excuse given for the beard policy is fit tests with respirators. Having performed fit tests for over twenty years, I can tell you a close beard does not alter a fit test. But the lawyers for the respirator companies have added clauses in their literature that says the wearer must be clean shaven. The clause in there to say that any wearer who gets injured was a mammal with hair and shouldn't have been wearing the respirator with two hours stubble on his face."

I didn't expect him to change his mind. This man would never change his mind. He's in charge and everyone needs to know it.

His face was getting red. He couldn't lose his captain veneer. That would mean I won. Bet he was going to scream into his pillow as soon as I left. I could feel my dismissal from his office coming.

"Doc, that's a very interesting, but extremely wrong, take on the situation. I don't want to hear another word on the topic, ever!"

"Now, please excuse yourself. I have work to do."

I got up and left. I made sure to chuckle out loud outside his office door. I wanted him to know that exchange was fun for me.

\* \* \*

The next morning at breakfast I sat at my usual spot to the left of the captain. He was already seated when I entered the room, face shaven, and head shaven, just like it was when I was a submariner.

The captain shook his head in dismay.

"What have you done to your head?"

"You want active duty. This is what I did when I was active duty. This is the real me. This is the warrior. I am now the warrior. This is what you want, this is what you get. I'll chew out every mariner with stubble. They're going to come crying to you to make me back off."

"If you're playing some kind of psychological game with me, it's not going to work. You can't piss me off."

Tatiana, who had been observing quietly, chimed in, "Spend ten minutes with him and he will."

The captain shot her a look that said shut the fuck up.

From that point forward, all meals were eaten in quiet or business only discussions, usually started by the captain.

The captain and I settled into an equilibrium. I did maintain the shave policy, though in private, I apologized to the crew for having to do so. They were understanding and quietly egged me on. I had become the face of the resistance.

Now resistance on a ship sounds like mutiny.

We weren't a munity; we were just a crew trying to maintain our morale.

We shaved. We obeyed all lawful orders. In fact, as far as I could tell, the ship did not suffer at all performance-wise.

I had become the moral resistance. My bald head had become a good luck charm. People would rub my head and say, "Thanks, Doc." I couldn't wait for Captain Stetson to leave, if just to grow my hair back and keep all those grubby hands off my head.

There were nights I struggled with my decision to 'poke the bear'. Captain Stetson wasn't an incompetent leader. He was just an ass, which I imagine is similar to what he thought about me. But in the end, we owe it to everyone one we serve with to make them better. In thirty years of experience, I noticed the best leaders trusted their subordinates and were confident in their ability to lead without reminding everyone all the time that they're in charge. I guess that was my true goal, to teach. Or, maybe I am an asshole who likes to stir the pot for my own entertainment. Can't I do both? At least that way, if I've failed at teaching the lesson, I've had a good time.

\* \* \*

Not everything was fun and games in my head. Especially not in medical.

Captain Stetson knocked on my door one morning, already agitated. "I need erythromycin eye drops," he barked.

That was... specific. "I haven't examined you yet. What do you need erythromycin for?"

"I have bacterial conjunctivitis." He said it like a man stating his blood type. "I need the drops."

I gestured him to the chair and gloved up. His left eye was slightly watery, pinkish, but textbook viral. "It's viral. No antibiotics needed. It'll resolve in a couple of weeks. Use these artificial tears for comfort, warm compresses a few times a day, and for God's sake wash your hands so you don't infect the other one."

He crossed his arms. "It's bacterial. I want the erythromycin."

"No. It's not, and no antibiotics for you."

His voice rose. "I'm the captain, and I demand you give me antibiotics! I've been through MEDPIC, I know what I'm talking about!"

I stared at him.

"You're seriously putting your two-week PowerPoint class up against my thirty years of experience?"

I took a deep breath. "You're the captain. Which means this is your medical space. Once I shut and lock this door, I can't stop you from breaking in and raiding the meds cabinet. But you are not, not, getting those drops from me. And your health record will say what I know it is: viral conjunctivitis."

I shooed him out, locked the door, and walked away.

The next morning, he was back. His left eye looked like a prolapsed rectum.

I couldn't help it, I laughed.

"Used the antibiotics, didn't you?"

"You could have warned me this would happen."

"I didn't know. I've never treated viral conjunctivitis with antibiotics before. Congratulations, you're a cautionary tale now."

He sighed. "You're enjoying this."

"No," I said, trying and failing to keep a straight face. "My job is to relieve pain, not cause it. This brings me no pleasure at all."

He blinked slowly, well, tried to blink, and asked, "What do I do now?"

"Same advice I gave you yesterday. But let me get a picture of this. There's a doc on the carrier who's heading into ophthalmology, he'd love this. I'll also get a second opinion about possibly starting you on a mild steroid drop."

To his credit, the captain nodded. "I'd appreciate that."

He left my office with something that might have been humility.

I waited two minutes, peeked down the passageway to make sure he was gone...and laughed my ass off.

* * *

The one thing Captain Brown did before taking leave was to barter with MSC headquarters over our route to the NAG.

Because we'd missed the Shellback ceremony earlier in the year due to weather and operational commitments, he had arranged for our official route to be south the of Maldives instead of the normal northern route. This allowed us to dip our keel into the Southern Hemisphere, cross the equator, and then turn north again. It was six hundred nautical miles out of our way, but we had the time, and to our surprise, Captain Stetson didn't try to change it.

Janice slowed our transit so we crossed the line at exactly noon on the day of the ceremony. That's precisely when the festivities began.

Believe it or not, in almost thirty years at sea, I had never crossed the line. The oldest mariner on the crew was a pollywog. Nobody, and I mean nobody, was more excited than me.

We gathered just aft of the mid-truck tunnel, where a makeshift throne made of pallets had been erected. Davy Jones sat elevated above the gathered shellbacks by a few feet.

Captain Stetson, in a rare moment of levity, agreed to play Davy Jones. He was offered to play King Neptune but didn't want to dress up for the ceremony. The captain looked different, almost happy. But it registered with me that he was going to enjoy the humiliation of the pollywogs.

For my part, I embraced my pollywog status. I had ripped up an old pair of jeans and a T-shirt. On my shoulder was a parrot made of finger splints and gauze bandages. I wore a patch over my left eye.

There were eighteen wogs, short for pollywogs, waiting to the side to be called forward by Davy Jones to entertain the royal court.

Davy Jones looked right at me and called me forward first. I got the sense he wanted to kick things off by embarrassing me.

"You with the silly bird, front and center."

I walked over and stood ram rod straight.

"The court asks that you entertain us. What is your talent wog?"

"I am a jester, a comedian if you will."

"Okay, jester, let's hear your lame jokes so we can get on with those with real talent."

I cleared my throat.

"Hi, I'm Jack and this is my parrot, Asshole. Say hello to the captain, Asshole."

And in my absolute best parrot voice, which was horrible, but somehow made it better, I squawked:

"Hello, Captain Asshole."

The court fell apart. The laughter was loud and hardy.

Captain Stetson leapt from the throne and declared, "The talent show is over. You have an hour to complete the rest of the ceremony, then back to work."

There was a moment of stunned silence as the captain stormed off. Then the crew laughed even harder than before.

I've said it before, and I'll say it again. If you can't laugh at yourself, it's my job to teach you how. This time, unlike with Nigel, I used my powers for good instead of evil.

We continued the abbreviated ceremony. Teddy stepped up as King Neptune.

I felt a little sorry for Teddy. He had worked hard on his costume, crafted a cardboard crown and trident scepter, and wore a repurposed bed sheet as a robe.

But he powered through. We had fun for an hour, then resumed our duties.

Nobody saw the captain for the rest of the day.

\* \* \*

The next morning, I was making rounds on the deck when I saw Teddy, Nigel, and Rachel chatting in the bosun office. I stepped into the doorway to say hello.

Rachel saw me first, "Welcome, nephew."

"Hi, Aunt Shirly."

Nigel gave me a high-five, "That was the most brutal takedown of a captain by a subordinate I've ever seen. That had to leave a mark."

Teddy added, "God, I hope I never get on your bad side. That was hilarious, but I don't carry cajones big enough to say that to a captain and I'm a licensed captain."

I thought about it for a second, "It wasn't premeditated. I felt he was trying to embarrass me, so, if the truth be told, I was just defending myself. Pre-emptively."

Teddy turned serious, "You need to back down now. Whatever started this pissing contest between you and the captain, it has got to stop. It's getting to the point where it's becoming counterproductive. I hope that was the last salvo from you. Whatever comes back at you, you just grin and bear it. Got it?"

"What, you don't think I can back down?"

All three of them said in unison, "No!"

I felt a light push between my shoulder blade, Janice. I stepped forward into the bosun office as she slipped into my place in the doorway.

I spoke first, "What brings the navigator all the way down from the ivory tower to mingle with us common folk?"

"I saw you on the deck and needed to come talk with you."

Everyone sat quietly, waiting for her next words.

"Captain Stetson is up on the bridge taking out his frustrations on everyone. If you thought he was an asshole before, he's morphed into something different, now he's a super asshole."

Still nothing from the rest of us.

"He chewed me out for charts that we've already sailed, routes in the rearview mirror. There's no rhyme or reason. He's just up there with a verbal flame thrower roasting anyone in his way. You did this. You go fix it."

Nigel spoke up. "Yeah, Doc, you might need to apologize. Not because any of us thought what you did wasn't a little bit warranted, but if he's up there tearing our junior personnel apart because of you, you might need to run interference. You've always said this was about crew morale. Well, now it's getting worse than it ever was."

Rachel agreed, "Yes nephew. If your goal is about improving morale, you'd better get up there and say you're sorry."

"I can't. I meant it."

Teddy put his hand on my shoulder. "They're not wrong. If the captain is going to go Godzilla on the crew, you're the one who pissed him off, you're the only one who can calm him down."

I shook Teddy's hand off my shoulder, "That's bullshit. You're second in command, Teddy. You calm him down."

"Nope. I'm not the one who took a giant crap in his corn flakes. That was you, my friend, you do it. I suggest you do it today."

Silence in the room.

"I'll tell you what," Teddy said, "I'll go with you as a witness, but I'm not saying a fucking thing. This is all on you."

* * *

Captain Stetson was at lunch in his usually place. The entire officer's mess was quiet. Everyone could feel the tension. This wasn't my goal. I just wanted him to stop messing up our carefully curated crew dynamic.

As always, I felt his goal was to prove to himself and his superiors that he was in charge. Well screw you, tiny man. True leaders lead by example not by being giant douchebags. That was my point, we're on his crew, but we were a far better crew before he showed up. He was messing with a good thing, and I personally resented it. Fuck you, Captain Stetson.

Teddy cleared his throat, "Doc, don't you have something to say to the captain."

"Not here."

The captain smiled, "If you want to apologize, I'll take it here in front of all the officers."

"No, I'm not going to apologize, but I do have something I'd like to talk to you about in private."

Teddy frowned. I could see him pleading not to throw gasoline on the fire.

The captain seemed intrigued, "What do you propose?"

"I propose that you and I have a private discussion in your office at 1315 with Teddy in attendance as a witness. That way it won't get out of hand."

"You think it's going to get out of hand?" He leaned in and whispered, "It's going to be a one-way discussion. You're going to listen and I'm going to talk."

I smiled, "You wanna bet?"

I was crossing all sorts of lines. Legally the captain at sea is solely responsible for the ship. Not the doc, not the chief mate, the captain. That's it.

I was breaking with all sorts of traditions and standards of behavior at sea. With that last comment, I might be in danger of breaking the law.

For certain, if I was still in the Navy, and not a civilian mariner, that was a chargeable offense under the USMJ (Uniforn Code of Military Justice). What rules it fractured as a civilian was fuzzy to me. Maybe I just get fired.

I paced in my stateroom until Teddy came and got me at 1310.

"You ready for this?"

"No."

"What are you going to say?"

"I'm going to request a transfer."

"That's chicken shit, Doc. Start the fire and then bail while everybody else gets consumed in it. That's bullshit and you know it."

"When what do you suggest I do?"

"Apology and leave it that. Take the ass chewing and move on. He wants your head on a spike. If it was 100 years ago, I might be sharpening an axe to remove your head."

I grabbed my throat.

"I'm not kidding. We'd throw your headless body overboard and swear it happened in an unexpected gale. Nobody would question it."

"Well, thank God, it's not a hundred years ago."

The captain was sitting behind his desk when we arrived. He didn't stand. There was no effort at being cordial. It wasn't expected either.

"Chief Mate have a seat. Doc, you stand and don't say a word."

I looked him in the eye. "If that's the kind of meeting..."

"Chief Mate, shut him up. Now!"

The chief mate, in a voice almost inaudible, "Doc."

The captain looked satisfied.

The only reason I kept quiet was out of respect for Teddy.

"I'm placing you on report. The paperwork is on my desk. Read it. Sign it. And then get out of my office."

I read what he'd written. It said nothing about the shellback ceremony. The report called me out for saying, "oh, yeah!" when he gave me an order. Damn if you're going to write me up, get it right.

"That's not what I said. I'm not signing this."

The captain started to get visibly upset. Teddy stood and whispered to me, "For God's sake, Doc, just sign the form. Get this over with."

Evidently the captain didn't like that Teddy wasn't 100% on his side.

"Do you have something to say Chief Mate?"

Teddy turned and faced the captain, "Permission to speak freely."

"Speak as you will."

"You may be the captain, and I can't say I agree with everything Doc has done, but you don't listen."

"What are you saying?"

"I'm saying you're an exceptionally smart person, a capable captain, but you're not the only smart person in the room. You don't know everything. From the day you stepped onboard this ship you've been hell bent on showing everyone just how smart and in charge you are. You're missing the point; you can't sail this ship by yourself. Other people know things. I have 15 years more experience sailing than you do. I'm rated a captain just like you, but I don't do it because I don't like the political bullshit with MSC headquarters. You do. Good for you. You've never asked me anything about me. I bet you've never asked any other person onboard what their qualifications are. I mean no disrespect captain, but you're the leader not the whole show. Learn to appreciate the contributions around you and then maybe Doc, in his misguided ways wouldn't have to call you an asshole in front of the whole crew."

The captain's eyes stretched wide open. "Is that all you have to say Teddy?"

"Yes."

The captain took a beat, "Doc, you can leave."

"Teddy, I'm placing you on report as well."

# Chapter 13—Fujairah, U.A.E.

A few hours after the visit with the captain, Teddy showed up in sickbay.

"Hey, Doc, how are you doing?"

"I'm fine. How about you?"

"Well, if I ever changed my mind about being a captain again, that ship has sailed."

"Pun intended."

"Yes."

Getting written up didn't bother me. It was a nothing burger for my career, no promotion, no demotion. I'm either an MSO or I'm not.

Teddy looked calm as can be as well. I had to ask.

"Why are you so calm?"

"Doc, I've been written up for less by much worse captains. I made my peace with being a Chief Mate a long time ago. I'm happy where I am. Besides, in a few more weeks John Brown will be back, and this will all be a bad dream."

"Good, I'm glad you're okay. It wasn't my intention to drag you into this."

"Here's some sage words for you. Don't wrestle with pigs. You both get dirty and the pig likes it."

"I think I was the pig in this scenario." I pushed my nose up and made an oinking noise.

He laughed, "You may be right."

"Tell me, Doc. Have you told anyone that you were written up."

"No."

"Don't. Let's see if the captain says anything. I'm betting he's waiting for the rumor mill to send the gossip back in his direction. Let's not feed his ego. Just let it go."

I shook Teddy's hand, "Done."

* * *

The coffee in the engine room still hadn't improved, so I braved afternoon coffee on the bridge. I caught up with Janice for a few minutes, and Scott Barlow wandered over. Somehow, Scott and I started talking baseball, specifically, how a pitcher's height affects how fast a pitch feels.

"My argument," I said, "is that the same 100 mph pitch from a 6'10" pitcher would feel faster than from a 6-footer. The taller guy's release point is closer to home plate, so the batter has less time to react."

Scott nodded, considering it.

Unfortunately, that's when Captain Stetson arrived.

He rounded the coffee machine like he was coming to relieve the watch late, overhearing just enough to get it wrong. "Ah, Doc. You're completely off base. When you're talking about relative vectors, both balls are moving at the same speed. That's physics.

"Yes, Captain. From one ball's point of view, their relative velocity is zero. I'll give you that," I said. "But I'm talking about it from the batter's perspective, how much time he has to react."

"No, Doc. You're wrong. I aced that topic at Mass Maritime. And I don't think you can hold a candle to me when it comes to relative vectors."

"No offense, Captain, but before I joined the Navy, I studied engineering at NC State for two years. I've taken more math and physics classes than you've had hot meals. And I know for a fact, you're wrong."

"I am not!"

I shrugged, the whole wrestling with pigs conversation freshly implanted in my brain. "Okay. You know better than me."

Satisfied, the captain walked away like he'd won a Nobel Prize in coffee shop physics.

I looked at Scott. "I'd trust him with relative vectors, but I don't think he could hit a fastball."

\* \* \*

Coming into the port of Fujairah, we picked up a Navy security team. They brought along .50-caliber machine guns and other toys meant to deter small boats from getting too close. They manned two posts forward and two aft. Compared to our ragtag crew of aging mariners, these active-duty sailors looked like they ate razor blades for breakfast.

The wide-open rules of the Western Pacific were over. We were now in the Middle East. Everyone was told to stay sharp.

As we approached the harbor, we passed at least fifty tankers sitting at anchor outside the shipping lane, each waiting their turn to offload or receive petroleum. We were classified differently, so we sailed by like we owned the place. Money probably had a lot to do with that.

Once we moored, port agents came aboard to lay down the rules. We were restricted to the port facility and the street adjacent to the pier. The only buildings we were authorized to enter were the duty-free shops and the Seaman's Club, unless escorted by someone with a port security badge.

This wasn't going to be a sightseeing port. We had three days to fuel, load cargo, and head back out to sea.

That first night, Nigel, Rachel, and I went to the Seaman's Club for dinner and a couple drinks. A Filipino cover band was playing their hearts out at the far end of the room, crushing one American hit after another.

During intermission, Rachel wandered off toward the stage and came back with a young woman who looked oddly familiar. Out of place, but familiar.

Rachel grinned. "Here's a hint: you spent all Christmas Eve with her."

I blinked. "Oh my God, Miranda? What are you doing here?"

She smiled and leaned in for a hug. I hugged her back, figured it would be rude not to.

When she stepped back, she said, "After Christmas, I took some time off from the club, and during that break, our band landed a four-month contract here. I haven't set foot in the Barrio since. That night with you was special. Thank you."

"I'm glad things are working out for you."

Nigel chimed in, "You should join us for a drink during your break."

"I wish I could, but I've got band stuff to take care of. I just saw your friend and had to say hello. You'll come back and watch us again before you leave, yes?"

We all promised we would, and we did. She sang. We listened. There wasn't much else to say. But it was good to see a young girl from the bars in the Barrio doing something else.

The next night, a Chinese naval oiler docked just ahead of us. That was a first for me, I'd never seen a Chinese ship operating this far from home.

At the Seaman's Club, it was our usual crew, plus Janice, who'd had duty the night before. The food was a mix of American and Middle Eastern. The beer was German. The crowd was mostly American, until it wasn't.

About forty Chinese sailors walked in. They saw the twenty or so Americans already there, paused, and then decided to take a table anyway. It was a semi-autonomous free port, and sailors are sailors.

I decided to approach the guy who looked like he was in charge, he wasn't in uniform, but he had that air about him.

"Do you speak any English?" I asked. "I don't know much Chinese, except shi shi."

He laughed. "I think you meant xiè xiè. You just said, 'shit, shit.'"

"Well, that's not what I was going for. Your English is really good, where'd you learn?"

"In high school, back in China. But I became fluent after I moved to Chapel Hill, North Carolina. I went to the University of North Carolina."

"No kidding? I went to NC State!"

He laughed again. "Now we are not only enemies because of different navies, but because of Moo U, I like you even less."

We both threw our heads back and laughed so loud the band actually paused for a second.

The Chinese sailors looked confused. The Americans looked confused. We didn't care.

I held out my hand. "John F. Davidson. Friends call me Jack."

He shook it. "Jian Zhang. When I was at UNC, my friends called me Jack, too."

"Well then, nice to meet you, Jack."

We grinned at each other while the rest of the bar just blinked at us.

The song ended. Jian Jack said something to his crew in Chinese. They all burst into cheers.

"What did you say?" I asked.

"Do you mind if I address your crew?"

"Be my guest."

He turned to the American tables and said, "American mariners, this is my new friend, Jack. You are now our honored guests. First round is on me!"

Then the Americans cheered.

The rest of the night was small talk, shared laughs, and rounds passed back and forth, one Jack to another.

\* \* \*

The next evening, the American and Chinese sailors passed each other on the street. Knowing smiles, hellos, and nǐ hǎos were exchanged. Nothing else needed to be said. Mutual respect achieved. Hopefully, we'd never have to find out how we'd treat each other in less ideal circumstances.

Janice, Teddy, and I had dinner at the Seaman's Club. Miranda came over to the table to say hello, which meant I had to retell the Christmas Eve story to doubting recipients.

"No, really, we just talked. Rachel and Nigel were my witnesses. I even told Chloé about it."

"Suuuure."

"You guys suck. Now my feelings are hurt."

We made it an early night; we needed to be up at 0500 to leave port tomorrow.

I snuggled into bed and had barely fallen asleep when Janice knocked on my door.

Why is it I'm always in just my shorts when Janice knocks?

"The Chief Mate wants all department heads in the lounge. Now. And for God's sake, buy some PJs."

It was only 2230. The meeting didn't make sense, especially not one called by the Chief Mate.

Not everyone had made it back yet; it was still early enough that some were enjoying their last night in port.

Once we'd gathered everyone we thought we were going to get, Teddy started the meeting.

"I'm going to come right out and say it. Captain Stetson left the port facility this evening with a woman. I don't know what happened, but he's being held by port security. Somehow, the Embassy is involved. I've been told that, effective immediately, Captain Stetson has been fired by MSC. I am now the acting captain. We still depart as scheduled tomorrow morning."

Nobody breathed. We didn't know what to say.

Chief Engineer Sam Smith finally asked, "How did this happen?"

Tatiana raised her hand.

Teddy said, "Yes?"

"I know how it happened."

A collective, "You do?"

"I saw him leave the base with the woman. I took a picture and reported him to security."

Everyone gasped.

"You all know he was an asshole. Doc plays his games. I play mine."

I said, "I was trying to teach him a lesson. You dropped a fucking building on his head. Holy shit, Tatiana, please tell me if I'm in danger of pissing you off."

"No. You're all safe. I only hit hard when it's necessary. I was happy to watch him screw up. But I was afraid to have him as our captain in the NAG."

Teddy took back the room.

"Wow. I don't know if I should thank you or run from you."

"That being said, we're going to have to transit the Straits tomorrow night. Nothing has changed in that regard. I've made a call to Captain Brown. He'll rejoin us a week earlier than expected, when we pull into Bahrain two weeks from now."

Teddy closed his eyes for a moment of reflection.

"I think we're done for this evening. See you tomorrow at 0500."

\* \* \*

We gathered on deck at 0500 for departure. Nobody looked rested. A few were squinting like they'd

154

slept in their work boots. Teddy had that combination of too much coffee and not enough certainty that every new leader wears like a name tag.

Rachel leaned over and whispered, "Do you think he's going to salute himself?"

I didn't answer. I was too busy wondering if Tatiana had slept at all or just spent the night pacing like a wolf with a clipboard. She stood off to the side, arms crossed, eyes sweeping the deck like she was still calculating something.

Teddy cleared his throat and said, "Good morning. We are underway in thirty minutes. Department heads, make your final checks and report to the bridge. I'll be there shortly. Let's keep it tight and professional, thank you."

Then he paused, like he couldn't believe he was the one saying that.

We broke formation like a middle school fire drill, everyone peeling off to their corners of the ship. As I turned toward sickbay, Janice walked beside me.

"Well," she said, "the coup d'état went smoother than I expected."

"Technically not a coup," I said. "More like an unexpected self-extraction."

"Still. You have to admit, Tatiana runs a cleaner operation than the CIA."

I looked over my shoulder at her. "Please don't say that too loud. She might hear you and start black-bagging people."

By breakfast, the story had already mutated. The captain had either been arrested for espionage, eloped with an Emirati princess, or defected to Iran. Janice voted for all three.

I stayed out of it. I'd seen Tatiana's photo.

We stood on the foredeck as the harbor pilot guided us away from the pier. The early morning air was thick with diesel and brine, the kind that sticks to your skin and your memories.

Stacked neatly near the end of the pier sat a pile of luggage and two garment bags. A folding chair had been added, like someone might come sit vigil. On top of the pile was a cardboard box marked in black Sharpie:

PERSONAL EFFECTS – STETSON

Nigel spotted it first. "Tell me that's real."

Rachel crossed her arms. "Very real."

I said, "They said they'd hold it until someone from the Embassy comes to get it."

"Bet it's mostly hair gel and regret," Nigel said.

Rachel snorted. "I bet they had to pack his ego in a separate box."

We watched it grow smaller behind us as the HUDSON cleared the harbor. No words needed. The man was gone. And nobody felt sorry for him.

# Chapter 14—Arabian Gulf

Crossing the Straits of Hormuz is a nighttime activity for MSC ships. Unfortunately, we couldn't just hog the pier space in Fujairah, other ships needed it. Our ideal scenario would have been to have a leisurely breakfast, lunch pier side and then sail straight to the straits.

Janice had picked out a box in the Gulf of Oman for us to do gator squares, a term used to describe a navy ship loitering at sea.

As we did two knots to nowhere, lunch was served.

The chow line seemed a little lighter today. Crew members were smiling. The cooks were serving the food with extra care. It was burger day. That was always a bit of a mood elevator. Or...just hear me out, maybe it was the sweet potato fries.

I couldn't quite put my finger on it until I saw Teddy sitting in the captain's chair at the head table. There was a full crowd around the table, unlike the last few weeks when people delayed eating until later in the hour.

I sat to Teddy's left.

"You look like a natural."

Teddy smiled.

"I mean, the way you're eating that burger makes me think you've eaten burgers before."

The whole table chuckled.

As we ate, Teddy asked a few business-related questions of his department heads. The conversation was free flowing and easy.

Once the meal was consumed, nobody left the table. Then Sam Smith asked Teddy, "Captain, don't you have something else you need to say?"

Teddy understood the assignment.

"Why did the chicken cross the playground?" He paused just long enough to give us a chance to answer. "To get to the other slide."

There were a few chuckles around the table.

Tatiana said, "If you don't come up with better jokes than that I'm going to send your picture to the Embassy."

We laughed so hard that it turned to tears and then somebody said, "weee" as the laughter died and we started laughing all over again.

\* \* \*

We entered the Straits of Hormuz as night fell. Extra hands were on the bridge. The engine room, which was usually automated for the night, was fully manned. We prepared for the worst, though I can't recall ever having an incident.

I stood on the bridge wing with Teddy. There is no role for the doc on the bridge, but hey, unless there's a spurting artery, sickbay can be a little boring.

"You doin' okay, Captain?"

I liked calling Teddy captain. He was worthy of the title.

He scanned the water with his binoculars.

"Yeah, thanks Doc."

He let the 'binocs' hang from their strap from around his neck. He was still using his same old set with the chief mate label on the side.

"Do you know why we're always on such high alert when crossing the Straits?"

I thought I might know the answer, but I was in listening mode, not talking mode.

"Especially when we're inbound to the Gulf, we're in Iranian waters. International rules dictate that in these instances where two international bodies of water are connected by such a narrow strait that free navigation is allowed. But there's a limit to how close we can get to the Iranian shores. And trust me, the Iranians watch our movements through here like hawks. Thus, we're fully manned and fully alert."

"Got it."

Then he added, "Plus all these fucking fish boats. Who fishes at night?"

Teddy walked inside to the bridge shouting some instructions I couldn't make out.

I stayed on the port bridge wing. After a day of hot Middle Eastern Sun, the darkness and breeze felt good. The lights of Iran were at the edge of the horizon.

My mind wandered. I thought, wouldn't it be cool to just pull into an Iranian port and send Nigel down to negotiate our stay in Farsi. I wondered how the Iranians would react to his mohawk.

A little daydreaming is good, but when I start to debate myself about fictitious mohawk reactions, it might be time for me to seek other stimuli.

For night navigation the lights on the bridge are set to red. Night vision is important. It helps you dodge fishing boats and avoid icebergs.

I found Janice with her red-lit head lamp over her chart table double checking our position regularly. She was all business with her dividers and ruler, drawing lines to compare our planned route versus the actual route. In the dim light it looked to me like the watch standers were spot on, far closer to the planned line than in the open ocean.

The dark demands low voices. The situation demands low voices.

I whispered to Janice, "The guys are doing great."

She whispered back, "Yeah, this new kid is a Maine Maritime guy. He's smart."

"I know there's a joke there between Mass and Maine Maritime, but why?"

"You have to ask? I hear you give anyone who went to or roots for UNC crap. It's the same thing. Though I do tend to think Mass puts out mariners that are cockier than they are talented."

"Like the captain that shall not be named?"

"Exactly."

She went to get the next plot point from the electronic nav panel followed by more plotting.

"How'd it go up here during the day while we were going in circles?"

"It was quiet and relaxed. I was able to focus on our plans for the next few days without looking over my shoulder."

"Did Teddy, I mean, did the captain spend much time up here?"

"No. I understand he was down on the decks and in the chief mate's office most of the day."

"Did he say anything to you?"

Right then I felt a hand on my shoulder. It was Teddy.

"Hey Doc, why don't you call it a night and leave my navigator alone. I'm fine. You don't have to worry about me."

"Okay, Captain." I paused, "But I'm not worried about you, just curious. To take command in the fashion you did can be highly stressful. Just checking to see if you were the same Teddy we love, with just a little captain-y flavoring added in."

"Well, here's a little captain-y flavoring. Get the fuck off my bridge."

"Aye, Aye, Captain!"

Not that Teddy could see, but I was smiling ear to ear as I stepped off the bridge. We were heading into a highly stressful few months and we now had one less thing to worry about.

* * *

During our next UNREP with the USS New York, it was a blistering hot day. This wasn't Midwest hot, this was Death Valley hot with the mercury busting out of the top of the thermometer hot. The noontime temperature was 126°F.

To keep the deck crew cool I had enlisted half the SUs to run water and iced towels to the mariners on deck and in the sun. Those on the deck wore long sleeves and T-shirts used as scarves over their hard

161

hats to keep the sun from their necks and faces. If anyone on the crew ever wondered about the way Arabs dressed in the heat, this was a real-life lesson they would never forget.

The USS New York is a San Antonio-class amphibious ship, with sailors, marines, and all the equipment it takes to land on a beach. The NEW YORK was a real live Uncle Sam's can of whoop-ass. And they need fuel and groceries to make it all work. We had plenty of both for them. That kind of volume took time to transfer. Thus, we were destined to be in the sun for a long time.

Sometimes when it gets hot, it gets stupid too. About halfway through the UNREP an Iranian gunboat, with a .50-caliber gun on its foredeck, started to hang around the after end of the NEW YORK.

Our security team went on high alert and the NEW YORK's marines were lining up in sniper-like positions on the fantail. The game of chicken was on.

The gun boat would move to the left out of sight from our guns and then around to the right out of sight from the NEW YORK's guns. And then the coup de grâce, they started to come between our ships, while the fuel hoses were still attached.

This didn't really add any danger to our crews, they were the ones positioning themselves in what amounted to a murder hole. They were placing themselves in a gauntlet. It was almost as if they wanted us to fire. Our crews held with great restraint.

I headed to the flight deck to be witness to the massacre firsthand. Nigel joined me.

The water between the ships was rough and the gun boat was getting rocked hard.

Nigel yelled something in Farsi. The gun boat backed off as if they heard him.

"What did you just say to them?"

"Well, I figured since they didn't have anyone standing on the deck with their .50-cal and they have all those antennas around their bridge, that they were listening to us. So, I simply said, 'That roughness you're experiencing is called the venturi effect. Any second now your boat's going to flip, and you'll become shark chum after passing through one of our props.' And then I called them the Farsi equivalent of dumbasses."

"Well, it seems to have worked. Look, they're completely leaving the area."

We watched them until they disappeared over the horizon.

"Have you ever thought about becoming a negotiator?"

"Not a chance. I live for this."

The UNREP finished without further incident. The crew was wiped out. After dinner, the usual hustle and bustle of overtime did not exist. Everyone was in bed recovering.

The next day I went to morning muster with the deck crew. Captain Stone, the rock our deck department is built on, started the muster.

"Gentlemen, I have great news. We have only two UNREPs today and it's only 105°F."

\* \* \*

The summer in the Gulf was hot, but even the deck personnel had nothing to complain about when compared to the engine room. The oilers were designed during the cold war with Russia and designed for operations in the North Atlantic. Thus, air conditioning in the engine room wasn't even a consideration. Add bathtub warm waters as insulation around the hull and the engine room literally becomes a pressure cooker.

My routine, even out of the desert heat, was to make at least daily rounds to the engine room. In the heat I had a more important reason, to make sure the engineers weren't melting, literally. One of my jobs was to perform heat stress monitoring and calculate how long the human body could safely endure the temperatures. In this case, it was 140°F, safe to work for fifteen minutes, followed by a half-hour recovery break.

This meant two things, work progressed at glacial speeds, and the engineers were always sweaty messes. Sometimes it would take three or four changes of clothes to get through a day. The engineers now owned the laundry rooms, figuratively.

The Chief Engineer could usually be found in engineering control, the only space in the engine room with AC.

"Chief, when are you going to MacGyver a solution to your heat problem?"

"I already have one in mind. I'm going to find Aladdin's magical lamp. First wish? Move this ship to the Gulf of Alaska. My second wish? That you were only half the smart-ass you are now. And third, a billion dollars. Everyone wishes for money, right?"

"First of all, Chief, half a smart-ass is still a hell of a lot of smart-ass. Second, I'd skip the Alaska wish, go straight for the billion dollars and buy ice."

* * *

We got the tasking while we were still wringing out our socks from the last UNREP. A stern refuel, off the coast of Kuwait, for a minesweeper.

A minesweeper.

Normally, a small vessel like this was an add-on, something you hit while already in the area for bigger ships. This was our sole mission, five hundred miles round trip for a minesweeper.

Apparently, nobody in the decision chain thought to ask why a vessel roughly the size of a well-funded yacht couldn't just pull into a marina, swipe a government travel card, and top off like a fishing boat. Instead, we were ordered to burn twenty thousand gallons of fuel to deliver a few thousand.

That kind of math only works in two places: Congress and purgatory. We were somewhere in between.

Since the minesweeper is so small, we couldn't hook it up to span wire and add tension. It would literally pull the boat out of the water. The other issue is our fuel hoses are 2.5 inches in diameter. Even if the probe would fit, it would take longer to shut the pump down than it would to fill the tanks. For this, there is a special procedure. It's called a stern refueling.

In a nutshell, we toss a small-diameter fuel hose, lashed to a buoy, over the stern railing and let it feed out far enough that the minesweeper can follow safely, without getting tossed around like a pool toy in our

165

wake. They fish the buoy out of the water with a boat hook and attach the hose to their tank. We pump fuel for a very short time, they cap the hose, and throw it back in the water with the buoy. We reel it in. Stern fueling complete.

One day up, one day back, just to refuel the maritime equivalent of a wooden-hulled VW bug.

Don't get me wrong, I've got nothing against minesweepers. I don't have the balls to do their job. But this just didn't compute in my logic box. I know I don't have all the information, and I'm sometimes glad I don't. Because if I did, I might be even more pissed. Gulf logic. Who can figure.

\* \* \*

We moored pier side at the Khalifa Bin Salman Port. In front of us was a British submarine. Being a submariner, I was intrigued.

I put a ship's coin in my pocket and proceeded immediately to their gangway. The brow banner read HMS Astute. She was a beauty. All my bubblehead senses were tingling.

I spoke to the gangway watch, "I'm the medical services officer from the American supply ship that just pulled in. Is your doc aboard?"

"I don't know. Let me check." He picked up the receiver of the callbox attached to the gangway. Before he dialed, "Why should I say you're visiting?"

"Just tell him I'm a retired U.S. submariner and I have a ship's coin for him."

He dialed.

"Hey, mate, I have a Yank up here says he's the doc off the American ship. Wants to give you a coin."

He hung up. "Hold on. Says he'll be here in a minute."

A tall handsome Brit hurried up the gangway, "Hey, mate, I'm MA Stu Dodd. Is there something I can help you with?"

"Nothing. I just used to be in your shoes, and I know sometimes being forward deployed you can have needs. Is there anything you need. I'll help anyway I can."

"No, we've only been away from homeport for a month. I'm still in good shape."

I palmed the coin and extended my hand to shake.

He shook my hand and recoiled just a little because of the coin.

"Oh, I've heard about this Yank tradition of passing around coins. I don't have one to give back."

"It's not required. I just wanted to say hello to a brother."

"I have an idea. Hold on. I'll be right back."

He disappeared into the sub and about five minutes later, he returned.

"I have the captain's permission to bring you aboard. Have you ever been in a UK submarine?"

"I have not. I'm excited!"

This submarine was much newer than the Ohio class and Los Angeles class submarines I served. Most of this looked the same until we got to control. It looked like a video game to me. It was so advanced I couldn't describe it to you if I wanted. It was just that far out of my comprehension.

"This is so cool. Thank you so much for showing me this."

The submarine captain poked his head into control.

"Is Dodd giving you the grand tour."

"Yes, sir. Quite a machine you have here. I'd definitely have to requalify submarines if I wanted to work on one of these."

"Dodd said you were submariner. Which subs?"

"GEORGIA and SPRINGFIELD for a relief stent. I actually came onboard the SPRINGFIELD for the first time right here in Bahrain about twenty years ago."

The captain looked over to Dodd, "Have you shown our American friend the best part?"

"Not yet, sir. That's the next stop."

The best part? I couldn't even imagine what they could be alluding to.

We made our way to the mess decks. Where the best part became self-evident. They had beer on board.

"Would you fancy a beer?"

"Is that a trick question? Yes, please."

We drank a pint and talked shop and medical training.

When the beer was gone, the tour was over. A fitting end to an unplanned event.

When we got to the gangway, Dodd held out his hand to shake. In his hand was the medical rank insignia. I shook and thanked him.

"We don't have coins, but I thought you'd like this."

"Thanks Dodd. I'll know right where I'm going to keep it. You guys take care. See you around sometime."

"Yeah, see you."

\* \* \*

Two days in Bahrain. That was all we had. While I was playing submarines, Teddy went to the airport with the ship's agent to pick up Captain Brown. At quitting time, I went up to the captain's cabin. Teddy and the captain were talking, but the door was open, so I felt invited.

I knocked, of course, protocol.

"Come on in, Doc."

"Welcome back, captain. I just wanted you to know you're taking over from one of the best relief captains I've ever worked with."

"I'm back a week early and that's not the story I've been getting."

"I wasn't talking about the captain who shall not be named. I was talking about Teddy. He's a hell of captain."

"Oh. Yes, you're correct. He did a hell of job under less-than-ideal conditions."

He looked toward Teddy.

"Captain Stone. It is my pleasure to relieve you as the captain of the HUDSON. You stand relieved."

They shook hands.

An evil grin came over Captain Brown's face.

"Chief Mate Stone. It looks to me that you've been negligent in your duties."

Teddy shot the captain a stern side-eye.

"We were just wrapping up. I'm going to take Teddy out to dinner at the officer's club, do you want to join us?"

We ate and told stupid captain stories for an hour. When the meal was done, that chapter was complete. We didn't even call him the captain who shall not be named. On the HUDSON he just wasn't thought of at all.

# Chapter 15—Dubai, U.A.E.

Jebel Ali is the commercial port that services Dubai. Its waterways, viewed from the south, would best be described as the shape of an upside down 'F'. The tag on the top left of the 'F' is where the US Navy resides. The port is deep enough to accommodate large draft ships, which include the biggest oil tankers and US Navy aircraft carriers.

As we pulled into port there was another MSC ship already pier side, the USNS Rock. Jeff Fisher's new ship.

Jeff showed up on our quarter deck just as soon as the gangway was cleared for visitors. This time I was called to escort him.

"What's going on, Jack!"

"Not much, still sorting through your shit. You left me a mess."

A lie. Jeff knew it was a lie. But our code demanded it be said. Compliments are somehow deemed as weakness.

He laughed, "It wasn't a mess, you're just too dumb to understand the complex organizational skills of a master."

The same old banter. The same shit I was getting raked over the coals for at home. I saw the pattern plain as day. I was Neo seeing the matrix.

Time to change tactics. Chloé was coming in a few days, and I could use the practice.

"This time between visits was less than usual. It's nice to get a double dose of you this year."

Jeff looked puzzled, "Yeah, it is nice to see each other again. It's been eleven months though."

"Seems like it was just yesterday we were drinking in that beautiful D-Gar Yacht Club."

"Me and some of the guys from the ROCK are going to the Seafarers Club tonight for our last hurrah before heading back to the WESTPAC. You want to join us?"

"I can't. I made an appointment at 1700 for a mariner with a bad tooth. He's young and a little out of his element, so I promised to take him."

"Your call, buddy."

"Maybe I'll see you in the Sand Box when you get back. I'll just be out there soaking up the Wi-Fi and drinking a few beers with whomever is hanging around."

"Later, loser."

And Jeff was off.

I wasn't lying. There was a mariner with a tooth problem. I just didn't have to go with him. He was at least a twenty-year MSC employee and could probably tell me more about the clinic than I could tell him. There was nothing hard about it. I just didn't want to deal with Jeff's drinking unless I was close enough to the ship to easily walk away.

I ate dinner on the ship. I turned down an offer to go out on the town with Teddy and Janice. I just felt like feeling at home.

I've spent enough time in the Sand Box that it had become a home of sorts. It was a large open area under thick tarps suspended between poles. Under the tarps, which shaded about 5,000 square feet, were picnic tables. Between every other pole were large fans with a water attachment that misted water into the air. It did a fair job. In the sun the temperature was 103°F, in the Sand Box it was 99°F. Doesn't seem like much, it was all the difference in the world.

Shops made of trailers and Connex boxes surrounded the Sand Box. Out of twenty-five or so stores, only three were open, a Subway sandwich shop, a giftshop, and a phone center. Everything else stayed closed unless a 5,000-crew aircraft carrier was in port.

The real draw to the Sand Box was Wi-Fi provided free of charge by the USO.

The tables were filled with people hiding behind open computers and lost in their headphones. About a dozen coolers filled with beer were littered about. Some people drank and carried on, but most were quietly soaking up whatever their computers were providing them.

I found Captain Brown sitting alone with a cooler and his computer. He wasn't immune to nerding out. He handed me a beer as I sat and then spun his computer around.

"Honey, this is the doc, Jack. Doc, this is my wife, Linda."

"Hi, Doc."

"Hi, Linda."

The captain spun the computer back around. "Now you know each other."

I could hear Linda, "Yeah, we're like best friends now. Thanks, John."

I left him to it and called Chloé. She answered groggy, still in bed in San Diego. We talked logistics. I'd booked her business class, thinking I was being thoughtful. She appreciated it but didn't hide her nerves about flying. We ended on "I love you" but it felt like a line reading.

The captain called it quits about 2100 and I was going to follow him shortly. Jeff returned, pickled as a gherkin. His shipmates looked slightly annoyed and happy to ditch him when he stopped to talk to me.

"S'up buuuddy?"

"Hey, Jeff."

He laid his head on the table and belched loudly. People nearby, even those with headphones on, looked in our direction.

He lifted his head, "You got any more beer?"

"Don't you think you've had enough?"

"I'm not a pussy like you. I'm a man dammit. I go out. I drink. I conquer." He looked surprised, "Hey, didn't Caesar salad say that?"

"No, Jeff. That's not exactly what Caesar said. But I'll give you a 'C' for effort."

"Effort starts with an 'E', the term is 'A' for effort. Oh, that's stupid."

Another loud belch. "Hey, let's drink more beer."

"No, Jeff, I'm walking you back to your ship."

I gathered my stuff into a backpack and put it on. I grabbed Jeff's arm.

He started yelling, "Rape, rape. I think this man wants to kidnap me and rape me. Avenge me ROCK. AVENGE MEEEE!"

One of his shipmates came over. I don't know who he was, but he had sway, even over drunken Jeff.

"Doc, shut the fuck up! You're embarrassing yourself."

Jeff's eyes got big, and mouth got small, "Oh."

Not another word was said. I helped the pissed mariner get Jeff back to the ROCK. As I watched him stumble up the gangway, I couldn't shake the thought, there but for a few choices go I.

I called it a night.

Two more days and Chloé will be here.

\* \* \*

The next night passed quietly. The captain had a driver in Dubai, just like in Subic. He invited Teddy, Janice, and I to join him at the Seafarers Club. The food was good, the conversation easy, but in my head, I was already at the airport waiting for Chloé.

If they noticed, they didn't say a word. They let me sit in it, love-struck, distracted, floating.

Mature friends. What a concept.

\* \* \*

The car I hired picked me up outside the gate to the Navy compound. We arrived at Dubai International at 1800. The 1830 ETA was confirmed by FlightAware. Air Emirates flight EK230 was on time, due at 1830. I found the correct baggage claim area and waited. Forty-five minutes to deplane and clear customs is speedy. Seemed like forever to me.

Chloé looked refreshed. We embraced.

"You look so good. How was the flight?"

"I can't tell you how much of a difference the business class seating meant. I was so comfortable the entire time. I feel rested. I slept about half the flight. You've ruined me. I'm never flying economy again."

175

We chatted and gathered her bags. The ride to our hotel was only minutes away. Our room at the Marriott Marquis Dubai Creek had a view of the Burj Khalifa. We dined at the hotel that first night and just reconnected.

Chloé loved the beach. For the next few days we spent time at Marina Beach during the day. I am a water guy, but my old bones aren't up to more than wading in the sea, a near miss in a riptide convinced me that swimming pools were now my speed. I wish I was a beach guy, it would make it so much more enjoyable for Chloé than to have Mr. Crabby barking in her ear.

I asked, "This is an awesome beach, don't you think?"

"Yes, it's a fine beach. We have a better one on base on North Island and it doesn't cost us $10,000 to get to it. If you would come home, we'd be there right now. I wouldn't have to listen to you complain about the sand blowing in your face. Back home we'd have all our stuff. You'd be under the umbrella, I'd be tanning, and if it wasn't a good day for the beach, we'd just come back tomorrow."

I started to respond, but she cut me off, she was on a roll.

"And it wouldn't be hotter than the surface of the sun. You'd be retired and I would see you every day. I'd cook for you. You'd do projects and read. Or you could bike. You've always said you wanted to bike. There are so many sights we haven't seen in the US or Europe. Instead, you drag me off to the Middle East."

Her rant was a gut punch.

"You don't want to be here?"

"Yes, I want to be with you. I think this is a nice city. It's beautiful, clean, and modern. But I'm tired of flying alone. I want to travel with you, not to you."

"But if I wasn't in the MSC, we couldn't afford to travel like this."

"If you weren't in the MSC, we wouldn't have to travel like this."

"So, you're saying you want me home? Why do I always feel like I'm intruding on your life when I'm home?"

"God, Jack. You're the smartest man I know…"

"You need to meet more people."

"Dammit, Jack. Don't be a smart-ass now. I'm trying to get through to you. I love you. I want you around. When you're only home eight or twelve weeks, and not consecutive weeks, you are basically an intruder in my life. You don't get it. You'd rather bounce around the world making stupid jokes with Jeff than be a family, be my family. The kids are grown. I'm all alone. You have your crew, but I'm alone. Even when we're together, you're somewhere else. Do you get it? Can I spell it out for you any more than that?"

I had so many things I wanted to say, but they all felt wrong in my head.

"See. Nothing to say." Tears began to roll down her cheeks.

"Do you want to go to Irish Village for dinner tonight?"

She didn't say a word.

She just shook her head while she gathered her beach towel.

* * *

We walked to the Irish Village from our hotel. It was only a matter of blocks. My tendency was to walk too fast for Chloé so I was mindful of my pace and especially my tone.

Dinner consisted of Fish and Chips and Guinness Draught. A fine meal wherever you happen to be in the world.

The conversation was light. Neither one of us wanted to wade into the discussion that ended at the beach earlier. Chloé and I were about to pay the check and leave when I heard a bit of a disturbance from across the restaurant. Near the bar were three HUDSON mariners harassing a young girl who was just trying to get a drink from the bartender.

"Sorry, honey. I can't let this stand."

She waved her hand for me to go. The look on her face was less than thrilled.

I approached the bar to a choir of, "Doc!"

I didn't respond in kind.

"It appears to me you guys aren't reading this young lady's signals. She doesn't want anything to do with you. Move along."

One of them spoke up, "We're just having fun. What, Doc? Didn't you ever have fun when you were young?"

I leaned in, "This isn't fun, at least it's not for her. Let's ask her."

I turned to the young lady, "Are you having fun?"

"No, sir. Can I go?"

"Of course. I'm sorry these young hooligans have disturbed your evening."

"Thank you." She disappeared around the corner of the bar.

"Leave her alone now. See you back at the ship."

I went back to Chloè.

"Sorry about that."

She said flatly, "Always so gallant."

We paid and walked towards the exit.

Seated near the exit at a high pub table was the girl from the bar and what appeared to be her parents. Surrounding them were the three HUDSON mariners. The mariners were laughing and carrying on while the seated patrons looked distressed.

"Sorry, Chloé. I can't let this go. I already told those clowns to leave that girl alone. I need to put an end to this."

I stepped up to the table and addressed the fatherly figure.

"Excuse me, sir, are these men bothering you?"

"Yes."

I face the HUDSON mariners. "Gentleman, I beg you to move on. If you don't, I'll make sure you swim behind the ship all the way back to the United States. Do we have an understanding?"

"Dammit Doc, mind your own business."

"Okay shipmate, let me put it another way. I'm going to have a long talk with the bosun tomorrow, unless you leave right now. At my request he'd be happy to ride each one of your asses until I say stop. And when he's not on you like white on rice, I'm going to find every reason that I can to harass you. Do you want that kind of attention in your life?"

179

The defacto leader of the group said, "We'll report you to the union."

I laughed, "Me and the bosun have already earned our retirements. They'd just make us retire. There's no downside for us. Try me."

They huffed and left the bar.

I looked to the young lady, "Again, I'm sorry for the inconvenience. If they come back just go the security office next door."

Chloé gently tugged at my elbow for us to head for the exit.

Before I could turn to leave the father said, "Please join my family for a round. It's the least we could do to say thank you."

"I appreciate that."

"Whatcha drinkin'?"

"Guinness please."

I could hear Chloé sigh. I could see the mother sigh as well.

The father and I talked for two Guinness. Chloé was as charming as could be with the women.

We learned they were on a high school graduation trip with their daughter. She had a fascination with Dubai, so that's where they came.

The walk back to the hotel was nice, but this trip hadn't turned out to be the romantic getaway I was hoping for. The fire I'd hoped for was barely an ember. I was praying it wouldn't go out.

\* \* \*

I was on my best behavior for the last trip to the beach. I didn't say much for fear of ruining it for Chloé. She seemed content.

The day passed quickly, and it was time for Chloé to head home.

I walked her to security, suitcase rolling behind us. She held her boarding pass in one hand, her phone in the other. We stood there too long, caught between wanting more time and knowing there wasn't any.

"I love our little vacations," she said.

"Me too. It was really good to see you."

She nodded but didn't move.

"I hate always flying alone."

I smiled. "Yeah, you said that the other day as well. Those flights aren't cheap. I'll try to plan better next time."

She blinked. Once. Twice.

"That's not what I meant. You keep missing the point."

I stepped in, trying to recover. "I just meant, I was glad you came. I thought the flight would make it easier."

"It's not about the seat, Jack."

She wasn't mad. Just done.

And standing there, watching her grip the handle of her suitcase like a shield, I knew it wasn't about the flight. Or the miles. Or the class of seat. It was about me; always thinking convenience could replace presence.

And I missed it. Again.

Her voice stayed tight, low. Not angry, but final.

"It's about the coming and going. One of us is always the visitor in the other one's world. I want more than phone calls and countdowns. I want a life with my husband that isn't measured in leave slips and hotel receipts."

"So you want me to quit?"

She didn't answer right away.

"I want you to want something else. I want you to want us more than you want this."

Her gate number flashed on the screen. She adjusted her bag and kissed me lightly on the cheek.

"I love you. But I can't keep loving someone, someone who doesn't love being home."

She walked through security without looking back.

I stood there until the screen said her flight was boarding. Then I turned and walked back into Dubai, where everything was shiny and nothing felt real.

# Chapter 16—Djibouti

The HUDSON was detoured from the Arabian Gulf to the Horn of Africa to support pirate interdiction duty. Talk about the proverbial frying pan into the fire.

The Arabian Gulf was hot, but at least between trips to sea we were treated to world-class amenities. There was always something to do ashore. Bahrain is the Las Vegas of the Middle East and Dubai is its New York.

Djibouti was like Death Valley with camels. I knew we weren't in Kansas, or Kuwait, anymore. The ship moored next to camel pens, the kind used to hold livestock before loading onto export ships. And as Chloé would say whenever we visited her family in rural North Carolina, usually just after the first wave of manure hit us: "Today, the farm is farming."

In Djibouti, the pier was farming every day.

Fun fact, your nose adapts. It registers the smell and then filters it out so your brain can focus on new, potentially dangerous scents. But it doesn't mean you stop breathing in camel shit twenty-four/seven.

Our job was to run the length of the Horn of Africa, refueling Navy frigates chasing pirates and looking impressive on the evening news. We did loops down the Somali coast, then returned to Djibouti every week or so for fuel, cargo, and to remember why we hated Djibouti.

No Chamorro Village. No golf course. Just two points of interest: the Djibouti Palace Kempinski, a five-star resort none of us could afford, and Camp Lemonnier, affectionately known as Camp Lemonade.

I never made it to the Kempinski, but rumor had it the steak there didn't moo when you cut into it. That alone made it seven stars above the port.

Camp Lemonade had the real prize: Wi-Fi. Which meant the coffee shop was packed with deployed personnel and desperate mariners trying to download updates or talk to family before the connection dropped.

* * *

I once ran into a hospital corpsman with a Marine expeditionary force. As sailors do, we swapped stories, and he gave me the best sea story I'd ever heard, which means it's probably 60% true and 100% worth repeating.

He was on a hump through undisclosed African brushland with a platoon. They passed a baboon sitting on a log, watching them pass like he was the commanding officer. One Marine decided it would be funny to put a Marine Corps T-shirt on the baboon. Someone tried to talk him out of it. The Gunny gave a direct order to leave the monkey alone. That should have been the end of it.

It wasn't.

The Marine pulled the shirt from his pack and stepped forward.

One punch.

That's all it took. The baboon shattered his jaw like he was cracking a peanut. Blood everywhere. The corpsman treated him while the baboon sat calmly in the tree line, ten yards away, just watching.

When he called in for a medevac, the dispatcher hung up, thought it was a prank. He had to call back and send a picture. The Marine got what he wanted: a photo with the baboon.

\* \* \*

Pirates weren't the threat most people imagined. They targeted soft vessels. We weren't soft. Our own armed security team, plus the .50-cals bolted to the deck, made sure of that.

Honestly, the most dangerous thing in port was the beer. And the forklifts.

Our last time in Djibouti, AB James Franklin got his foot run over by a 12,000-pound forklift. He was wearing steel-toed boots, so his toes were intact, but the edge of the steel folded like a can lid into the top of his foot, fracturing all five metatarsals.

We had no ship van. Taxis weren't allowed on the pier. That left us a quarter-mile hike to the gate, which is a lot when your patient has only one working leg. I didn't think to grab the crutches from the ship's locker. So I became the crutch.

At first, we hobbled. Then his good leg gave out. I slung him on my back like a rucksack and started hauling. We passed guards, fences, a thousand parked cars, and not a single soul offered a ride.

I was pissed. Still am.

X-rays at Camp Lemonade confirmed the obvious: all five metatarsals were fractured. The Navy doc wanted an orthopedic consult, just in case of emboli. Not likely, but she wasn't wrong. She arranged a same-day consult at Bouffard French Military Hospital.

The clinic provided a driver to the gate. I flagged the first taxi I saw, negotiated the price, and off we went.

About two blocks in, the driver leaned back, holding a twig with leaves.

"You want khat?"

Khat's a stimulant leaf chewed by the locals. This guy's teeth were a monument to years of heavy use. We declined.

We were told the hospital was twenty minutes away. Forty-five minutes later, we were still weaving through town like he was lost or stalling. He kept mumbling in what I assumed was Somali.

I leaned in to Franklin. "If we hit a border checkpoint, jump."

Then, suddenly, we turned a corner and rolled straight up to the French military gate.

The driver smirked. "Same price for return," he said.

Inside, the ER was empty except for two nurses. They took vitals and called the surgeon. We waited forty-minutes, probably while he finished his espresso and cigarette.

The French doc entered, looked at the foot for maybe twenty-seconds, said, "Okay," and walked out. That was our consult.

I risked being held for ransom and heatstroke for a French shrug in a lab coat.

They rewrapped the foot, handed over crutches, and our khat-happy cabbie got us back to the pier in fifteen minutes flat.

I started the medevac paperwork. Crutches and ships don't mix. He couldn't stay. All we needed was approval to fly him home.

The day wasn't over. The paperwork would take hours. But the ship was sailing soon. We had a schedule to keep.

And MSC doesn't wait for broken feet.

\* \* \*

That night, all our comms went dark. Internal ship systems were fine, but anything off-hull, phones, email, even radio, was gone. Silence. Dead air.

Tatiana called every five minutes for an update. I had nothing. Just told her to standby, that someone would have to approve it soon. But nothing came.

Without admin approval, Tatiana couldn't book the ticket. The only other option was for Franklin to pay for it himself and hope for reimbursement, something no young AB in his right mind would do.

The tugs were tied. Gangway still down. Departure was imminent.

Franklin stood by the gangway, bags packed, crutches under one arm, medical records in hand, waiting for the trip home he'd already imagined.

I called the captain.

"We've got nothing. I say we err on the side of caution and take him with us. It's only a few days to Souda. We'll have it sorted by then."

"Agreed," he said. "Tell Franklin sorry, but he's with us for now. I've got other fires to put out."

Franklin didn't flinch.

"Hey, no biggie," he said, smiling. "I've got my PS4 and Call of Duty. I'll be fine."

And that was that. The gangway came up. The tugs pulled. Djibouti faded behind us.

We were northbound for the Med. And I had the sinking feeling the real fight hadn't started yet.

By mid-afternoon the next day, comms were restored and email came flooding in. Buried in my inbox was an approval for AB Franklin's medical repatriation and travel arrangements, timestamped 0300. Six hours before we left port.

Too late.

We were underway, and frankly, if he'd broken his foot at sea, nobody would've blinked.

But Captain Roberts did. Hard. The new Chief of MSC Medicine, freshly minted and still shiny, took it as a personal affront. I found out the hard way, when he called the ship directly.

It was the middle of the night EST. The call came into the captain's office. Captain Brown got me up there, handed me the phone, and stepped back like he was tossing me into a boxing ring.

"MSO Davidson," came the clipped voice. "I don't know what makes you think you can override my orders. I instructed that AB Franklin was to be left behind for medical repatriation."

"Sir, I understand, but we had no comms at the time,"

"I don't care about your communications failure. You were instructed to follow orders."

"With respect, Captain, I made a call based on the information I had,"

"I'm extremely upset with you. This was not your call to make."

That's when I snapped.

"Shut up and listen."

There was a beat of silence.

"How dare you talk,"

I hung up the phone.

Captain Brown blinked. "Was that the same thing you pulled on Captain Stetson?"

I didn't answer that. Instead, I growled, "Captain Stetson was a peach compared to this guy. I've been hearing stories about Roberts through the MSO grapevine for a month. If anything, they underplayed what an ass he is."

Roberts wasn't a clinician. He was a researcher in a uniform, one who'd never worked outside a lab or clinic, let alone in a war zone or on a ship.

The next day, my phone rang in medical. It was Roberts.

"You were extremely insubordinate last night. You know you operate under my medical license?"

"Yes, Captain. Revoke it."

"I just might. You had no right to overrule my decision."

"I didn't overrule anything. I didn't know about your decision until we were already out of port. I had minutes to decide. You've had a day and a half to second guess me. I stand by my call."

"I don't agree. A fracture doesn't belong onboard."

"Agreed. But if I'd left him and your order had been to keep him, I'd be answering for that. So I acted. I didn't have time to guess what you might say from a thousand miles away. Why are we even still talking about this?"

"Are you questioning my logic?"

"Yes."

"I'm a captain."

"I've met captains I wouldn't trust to lead a Cub Scout pack to chow."

"I don't like your tone."

"I'm sorry about that, Captain. But you're demanding I respect your judgment without offering the same in return. This wasn't easy. But I was there, and I made the best call I could. Please, let's move on and focus on the mariner."

Silence.

"You hung up on me last night."

"That was an accident. I dropped the phone."

We ended the call there. But he wasn't done.

The next day, same time, same number.

"MSO Davidson, are you ready to apologize to me?"

"For what?"

There was no 'sir,' no deference left.

"For overriding my decision and hanging up on me."

"I already explained, I didn't override anything. In the absence of orders, I made a call. That's what submariners do when there's no comms."

"You seem to forget, you're not on a submarine."

"For the amount of support I was getting, I might as well have been."

He paused.

"Listen, Captain. I'm not trying to be insubordinate, and I'm not trying to piss you off. I'm trying to take care of my crew. Franklin's okay. He's onboard, stable, and healthy. On the HUDSON, our world is right. Can we please just move on?"

"You don't tell me what to drop. You work for me,"

I hung up.

Then I called his Master Chief.

"Bill, if you don't get your boy under control, I'm gone next port. One more call about this and I'm finished."

"Jack, calm down,"

"No. Test me. One more call and I'll jump over the side mid-Suez and swim for shore."

I wasn't bluffing. Not really.

"Jesus, Jack. Why do you let him get under your skin?"

"Because I've got things to do, and he's wasting everyone's time."

That was the last call about Franklin.

But it wasn't the last I heard from Captain Roberts.

* * *

I've never questioned whether I wanted to keep going. Not really.

But this, this was different.

Like an alcoholic looking at a drink and feeling nothing, this was the first time I looked at the MSC and felt like I'd had enough.

These things run in cycles. Captain Roberts had two years to oversee MSC Medical, then he'd move on to his next post. I'd been playing this game, Navy and MSC combined, for nearly thirty.

This too shall pass.

And screw Captain Roberts.

# Chapter 17—Souda Bay, Crete

It was my first time transiting the Suez Canal, and I'd love to say it was exciting. It wasn't. It's a ditch. Through the desert. Sandy Egypt to the port, Sandy Sinai Peninsula on the starboard. That's it.

A few scattered concrete structures still showed scars, divots from bullets, maybe from the Six-Day War. One sand dune had a sign wedged into the slope that read Welcome to Egypt, which felt oddly cheerful considering the setting. We followed a U.S. aircraft carrier through the whole way, which was probably the most interesting part.

Once we were firmly into the Med, we offloaded the security team onto another MSC ship heading southbound. I felt a little bad for them. Hours on the deck, baking in the sun, watching for a threat that never comes. Just like most things in the military: boring...boring...AAAHHH!!, then back to boring.

\* \* \*

We had a few UNREPs in the Eastern Med over the next week, and then, Souda Bay.

Souda is practically a second home for MSC ships. We pulled in so often the local bars and restaurants treat us like returning family. Opa!

One of my greatest shames as a world-traveling mariner can be summed up in a single joke:

What do you call someone who speaks two languages? Bilingual.

What do you call someone who speaks only one? An American.

If it stings a little, that's because it's true. And that's why it's funny.

My Greek, like my Japanese, my Thai, and my Italian, consisted of thank you and please. Usually said in response to someone speaking English to me. That disconnect only hits me from time to time. I don't dwell on it, which is probably why I'm still not a polyglot.

* * *

Before we could blow off steam, we had business to wrap up.

AB Franklin had endured his time as a cast-wearing mariner without complaint. He was a model prisoner... err, shipmate. He finished his Call of Duty campaign and then powered through several other PS4 games while living the life of Riley in his stateroom.

Tatiana and I helped him to Chania International Airport, which shared an airfield with the U.S. Navy base. Since we had the captain's car and driver, we helped ourselves to the convenience, stocking up on supplies at the NEX and commissary.

When we returned to the pier, the workday was over. The sirens were no longer at sea. They now resided in the Argonaut.

It sat just fifty yards from our gangway, clean, air-conditioned, and offering the crew's three favorite things: beer, food, and Wi-Fi. Listed in order of priority.

Moored behind our stern was a submarine. I'd missed it earlier when we pulled in, but there she was, plain as day. What a beauty, too. The era of brow banners had long since passed, so I had no idea what boat it was, but I knew exactly where to find out.

194

The whole gang was already gathered at the picnic tables out front of the Argonaut, surrounded by sailors from the sub. About half of them were wearing T-shirts or ball caps with the word Georgia across the front.

Before even acknowledging my crew, I raised my voice and called out,

"Somebody tell me quick, Blue Crew or Gold Crew?"

"Blue Crew!" someone shouted.

My grin stretched wide. "Hell yeah! Gold Crew sucks!"

Gold Crew didn't actually suck. It was just one of those submarine traditions, a friendly rivalry unique to the SSBNs.

While I had their attention, I called out, "Where's your doc?"

A woman with auburn hair and two full sleeves of tattoos stood up from the far end of the table.

"That's me. Who's asking?"

I completely forgot my own crew existed. I walked straight over, hand extended.

"Jack Davidson. 729-Blue. I was on her in the late '90s. I'm sure there've been a few docs between you and me."

She shook my hand. "Believe it or not, your name still floats around, seen it on a few old documents. HMCS Pam Kowalski."

It was a little strange, talking to a female submariner. They didn't start integrating boats until after I retired. But she was solid, professional, sharp, and I could tell: tough as nails. The kind of person you'd want holding the med bag when everything goes sideways.

Captain Brown came over. "Hey Doc, we were gonna head over to Loukoulos for dinner. You in?"

"Hell yes I am," I said, already half-turned toward my crew.

After saying goodbye to Pam, I headed off with the gang.

There was a smile tugging at me the whole walk. It felt good, knowing someone like her had stepped into the role I'd left behind.

\* \* \*

Loukoulos sat right on the water, just across the narrow road from a beach scattered with umbrellas and sunbathers too content to move. The place looked like someone had drawn a line between paradise and the pier, and we just happened to be on the winning side. Our table filled fast with calamari, dolmades, saganaki, and whatever else the kitchen could throw at us. Ice-cold Mythos bottles clinked like medals being handed out after a battle well-fought. Nobody said it out loud, but this felt like something earned. The kind of meal that makes you forget what day it is, and makes you hope tomorrow doesn't come too fast.

The sun was dipping low, casting gold over the water, but our table at Loukoulos was still in full blaze, bottles sweating, plates scraped clean, voices rising over one another like gulls.

Teddy was already two beers in and halfway to becoming a Mythos philosopher.

"I'm telling you," he said, stabbing at piece of octopus like it owed him money, "if this whole maritime gig goes sideways, I'm opening a restaurant. I'll call it Chow. Rustic charm. Terrible service. Absolutely no tipping."

Rachel leaned in. "Oh, that exists. It's called the Chief's Mess."

Everyone laughed. Even John, Captain Brown, but off duty now, wearing a linen shirt that looked like it hadn't seen a uniform collar in weeks, cracked a smile.

"You'd have to cook something first," Janice added, poking Teddy's shoulder. "You think dry cereal counts as cuisine."

Teddy gave her a wounded look. "That was one time. One time I forgot to add water to the oatmeal."

Nigel raised his glass. "To undercooked oats and overcooked sea stories."

We clinked glasses, the sound sharp in the evening air.

"Speaking of stories," Rachel said, turning to me, "remember Singapore? The roach, the bathrobe, the fire alarm,"

"No," I cut her off. "Absolutely not. We're in paradise. That story stays buried like cursed treasure."

"But it's so good," she grinned.

"And cursed," I said, pointing my fork at her. "Let me have one peaceful dinner without reliving the worst week of my life."

"Fine," she said, mock-sulking into a grilled calamari ring. "But it's coming out next port."

John raised his glass again, slower this time. "To those not with us."

The table quieted. Just for a breath.

"To Buckley," Nigel said.

We drank, not solemnly, but meaningfully. That was the trick of it. You don't toast the dead with tears. You toast them with stories and food and sun on your face. That's how you make it count.

The silence didn't last long. Janice was already nudging Teddy about something, and he was defending himself in pantomime. Nigel pointed out a boat moored in the bay and rattled off the builder, tonnage, and hull material like he was the one who launched it. Teddy still bet him five euros he was wrong. Rachel ordered another round. And John leaned back, watching it all with that quiet approval that only a good captain, or a good friend, can wear without trying.

I let it all wash over me. The plates, the drinks, the voices rising and falling like a tide. For one night, we weren't under way, or on duty, or in uniform.

We were just a crew.

And for now, only this moment mattered.

* * *

The next day, during afternoon coffee on the bridge, I heard a voice behind me.

"Hey Doc."

I turned. The face was familiar. The voice too. The name, gone.

My bespectacled friend from the USNS Used-to-Sail caught the look in my eye.

"It's Tom. Tom van der Sterre."

"That's right!" I said, like he was the one who'd forgotten his own name.

"To be fair, Doc, I only remembered Doc. What's your name again?"

We shook hands. "Jack Davidson. How long's it been?"

"About five years," he said. "Long time. How've you been?"

Coffee turned into a conversation that ran long past regulation caffeine allowance. That's what happens when old shipmates roll back into your life.

Tom was a stargazer. Literally. He traveled with a telescope in his seabag and treated it with more reverence than his rack. He was our personal Neil deGrasse Tyson: smart, funny, personable, and just nerdy enough to lose us halfway through a sentence. But he never left us behind, when we got lost, he circled back, explained it again, and somehow made us feel smarter for asking.

His patience for our ignorance was... well, cosmic.

Tom's other passion, one I shared wholeheartedly, was naval history. We'd formed our own informal book club, swapping titles from the crew's library and dissecting them like we were defending thesis papers on the quarterdeck.

My usual snarky BS still made appearances when Tom was around, especially on the bridge, but never at him. He was like an anti-snark catalyst. Something about his presence made me keep the edge sheathed.

Truth was, I liked who I was when he was around.

\* \* \*

The other new crew addition in Souda was a shipmate from my last ship, and someone I'd been missing since this odyssey on the HUDSON began.

Rufus Carmichael, First Engineer, was the architect of the engine room coffee mess I'd bragged about. It took him a few weeks to whip it into shape, but he did it. My morning coffee routine now included a stop in engine room control.

Rufus had played college football and even had a cup of coffee with the Arizona Cardinals before turning maritime engineer.

Now in his forties, he hadn't lost the physique. He still looked like a running back who could hit a hole and make linebackers think twice. His bench press at forty beat mine in my prime by a hundred pounds. These days, it beat me by two hundred.

But Rufus was no stereotype. Despite the build, he was cerebral, sharp, steady, and deliberate. He was funny, but never a clown. Quiet, but never hesitant. In every way, he was the big dog in the room. The rest of us? Yappy little mutts he tolerated.

"Hey Rufus," I asked one morning, "why'd you leave the Laramie?"

"I thought the chief engineer was going to retire. When he changed his mind, I had to find another path to chief."

"You could've gone the relief engineer route."

"Nah," he said, sipping his mug. "I don't want to fix other people's messes. I just want a home of my own. Sam says he's retiring in a year. So now I'm here."

I raised my cup of perfectly engineered coffee. "Here's to you making chief."

For the next few months, the HUDSON bounced around the Med, Crete, Augusta Bay, Italy, and the Aegean Sea, UNREPing and VERTREPing the whole way. Nothing out of the ordinary. Just professionalism on the high seas.

Then came the medical storm, proverbial, not literal.

The first issue came when a mariner checked onboard with an active case of chronic cellulitis in his lower leg. He'd been battling it for two years while working on an MSC tugboat out of Norfolk.

I requested his repatriation the day he arrived. His lower leg was at least 25% larger than the other, red, hot, and sporting pitting edema. Nice guy, but he belonged at sea the way an elephant belongs in a tree.

Unknown to me, Captain Roberts had outsourced the medical pre-screening for sea duty, to people who had no clue what sea duty meant. So, Roberts and I were back on the phone.

"This guy can't be out here," I said.

"He was screened just last week," Roberts replied. "He stays. Place him on antibiotics and move along."

"His job requires long periods of standing. He can't stand without swelling and pain. He needs proper treatment."

"It's chronic and managed."

"Have you even laid eyes on this guy's leg?"

"No."

"Then why aren't you listening to the one person who has? This is more than chronic, it's an active infection, and it's been active since before he got here. He needs real treatment."

Roberts paused. "No. He stays. Besides, you're not a doctor, and you don't have a diagnosis from a civilian physician to justify repatriation."

We went round and round, for weeks. The mariner's leg only got worse while we stayed at sea. He couldn't stand, so he couldn't work. And there was no doctor onboard to satisfy Captain Roberts' paperwork obsession.

The mariner suffered while I did everything I could to stop it. But if two years of specialists in Norfolk hadn't fixed it, what was I supposed to do with a limited formulary on a ship bouncing around the Med?

The episode ended when the mariner spiked a fever of 103°F. That was the one sign Captain Roberts couldn't ignore.

We happened to be near an aircraft carrier, and he ordered a helo medevac.

I never found out how it ended, just that a mariner was denied treatment for two weeks because of ego.

\* \* \*

After our final stop in Souda, just before heading to the maintenance period in Trieste, a young female mariner came to me, worried she might be pregnant.

I tested. She was.

No big deal. Women get pregnant all the time. It's happened at least eight billion times in the last hundred years.

The issue? She'd had an IUD placed just the week prior while we were in port. That meant an elevated risk of ectopic pregnancy. Not astronomically higher, but higher. Enough to warrant caution.

The cause for concern was no reason to panic. She had no signs or symptoms of an ectopic pregnancy.

But the same doctor who didn't care if a mariner's leg fell off was now hyper-concerned about this pregnancy.

"Is the IUD still in place?" Captain Roberts asked.

"I don't know. The patient is refusing a vaginal exam."

"Well, you have to verify."

"I can't. She's flatly refused several requests. I'm not going to ask her again."

"You're not fulfilling your responsibilities as a clinician."

"What do you want me to do? I can't hold her down and forcefully examine her. I believe there's a name for that... oh, yeah, rape. No exam. Period."

My warped brain laughed a little.

No period either, which is why we're here.

The situation resolved itself the only way it could, with Dr. Roberts painted into the corner of the correct answer.

We detoured toward Augusta Bay, and a helo from the base flew out to meet the ship. The pregnant mariner went ashore via medevac.

Nothing more was said, but my respect for MSC medical, with Captain Roberts in charge, sank a little further into the abyss.

I'd like to say that was the last time I questioned Captain Roberts. But I'm not a very good liar.

# Chapter 18—Trieste, Italy

Six months had passed since I had seen Chloé in Dubai. We talked every day, whether I was in port or at sea, but it wasn't enough. My body was getting tired and so was my mind.

A week in Trieste with Chloé would be just what I needed to fill my tanks again and get me through to the finish line in Norfolk. To be part of the three-quarter-world cruise. To complete the mission and transfer the ship from the West Coast to the East Coast. John was doing it. Teddy was doing it. Nigel was doing it. Rachel was doing it. Hell, everyone was doing it and I'm a part of everyone.

Was it FOMO, the fear of missing out? Was I afraid to see pictures on social media of all my Navy and MSC friends continuing to circumnavigate the globe while I relaxed in San Diego? They all had their own Chloé, but they kept going. The question has always been there, and the answer was always, just one more time. One more unknown to see.

\* \* \*

At morning coffee in engine room control, the captain and I were joined at the break table by the Sam and Rufus.

Sam spoke, "It's funny how suddenly you two have become regulars down here. I wonder what changed."

The captain spoke without taking his eyes off the coffee he was admiring.

"Sam, I thought you were smarter than that. Rufus has a much better personality than you. I kind of resent that you made me spell out the obvious and now I'm happy to know when you leave next year, there will be an upgrade in your position."

Rufus shrank from the compliment.

I let a chortle out and nearly passed coffee through my nose.

Sam just shook his head.

"After all we've been through, John, you're gonna treat me like that?"

"For a good cup of coffee, Sam, I'd throw you from the fantail."

Sam laughed, "You'd have to have Rufus' help to get my fat ass over the rail!"

Rufus got serious, "You guys can leave me out of your silly little verbal games. I ain't touching any of this conversation with a ten-foot pole. Am I right, Doc?"

I laughed, "I'm with the captain, I'd toss him overboard for coffee."

Rufus shook his head, stood and went to find saner things to do.

\* \* \*

We pulled into Trieste early the next morning. The harbor was calm, wrapped in a faint mist that clung to the hull like a memory not ready to let go. I stood at the rail as the mooring lines hit the pier. No fanfare. Just another port on the list.

But this one held more excitement. Chloé and I had lived in Italy for years, but never made it to Trieste. This one was an Italy bucket list item.

I watched the gangway go down and checked my phone again. FlightAware showed her flight was on time and currently located over the Eastern Atlantic Ocean. Chloé's flight wouldn't arrive for several hours, and I still had a train to catch.

By 0900, I was off the ship with my backpack slung over one shoulder, passport in hand, wearing civvies that still smelled faintly of ship oil no matter how many times I washed them.

At the station, I found a window seat on the Frecciarossa to Venice. The ride would be just under two hours, enough time to try and shift gears, to be something closer to a man again instead of just another smart-ass in a floating machine.

Out the window, northern Italy rolled by in shades of green and terracotta. Vineyards. Cypress trees. The occasional chapel steeple piercing through fog like it had business with the heavens.

I tried not to think too hard. No diagnostics. No assessments. No clocks or countdowns. Just breathe. Just be.

When we reached Venezia Mestre, I grabbed my backpack and stepped onto the platform. The humidity hit me first. Then the scent, brine, old stone, and espresso.

The airport shuttle was already boarding. One more leg.

One more stop before I saw her again.

\* \* \*

She walked out of customs in that slow-motion way that only happens in movies and reunions, like the universe itself agreed to pause and let me take in the moment. Chloé didn't run. She didn't shout. She just smiled and walked straight into my arms like it was the most obvious destination in the world.

I buried my face in her hair and inhaled. Home.

No words. Just a squeeze. A double pat on my back from her, our little signal that this hug had roots. Then, as if to reset everything I had been carrying, she whispered, "Hi."

That was it. I was okay again.

We stayed at a small hotel in Mestre, the mainland part of Venice that tourists usually ignore. Not us. We'd learned years ago that a cheap, clean room with good espresso and quiet hallways beats a five-star hotel if it means we sleep soundly and can walk to the train.

The first night, we did nothing grand. Dinner at a trattoria around the corner. House red wine, seafood risotto, and bruschetta so good it shut us both up. Then a short walk. Her hand in mine. Streetlamps reflecting off rain-soaked cobblestone. No expectations. No forced conversation. Just time doing what it does best, passing when you're not watching it too closely.

The next morning, we took the train across the lagoon into Venice proper. Our fifth visit, and yet it felt brand new. Maybe it was the time apart. Maybe it was the calm between us. Or maybe Venice just has a way of rearranging its magic, so it always feels like the first time.

We stepped off at Santa Lucia station into a world that didn't make sense. Boats instead of cars. Laughter echoing off buildings too old to still be standing. Pigeons staging coups in open piazzas. The scent of seaweed and espresso and pastry, every inhale a contradiction.

We didn't have an agenda. That was the point.

We walked.

And walked.

And walked.

Over bridges and through alleys that narrowed until we had to turn sideways to pass. Past shops filled with leather-bound journals, Murano glass, and overpriced masks that tourists bought pretending they'd use them back home. Through a quiet courtyard where laundry hung like festival flags above our heads. We stopped for espresso twice. Gelato once. And once, just because the sun hit her face in a way that made me forget what time it was.

We didn't argue. Not even once.

Unlike Dubai, where the pressure cooker of being together after too long apart had set us both off. Back then, we'd tried too hard to make the visit "perfect," and ended up weaponizing jet lag, expectations, and three days of silence. But not this time. We knew better now. There's a kind of grace that comes with age, or maybe just exhaustion. Either way, we left the armor at home.

Near sunset, we found a gondolier who didn't speak much English and didn't need to. He waved us aboard like he'd been expecting us all day. The water lapped at the sides as we drifted through canals that looked like paintings. Past shuttered windows and balconies with potted geraniums. Lovers kissing beneath laundry lines. Life suspended in mid-sentence.

Then we turned into the Grand Canal and there it was, Rialto Bridge rising like a stone rainbow.

The gondolier slowed as we passed beneath it. Tourists snapped photos. We didn't. We just held hands. I glanced at Chloé. She was already looking at me. No words. No big moment. Just the click of two people who still recognized each other beneath all the layers of fatigue, routine, and long-distance nonsense.

I said, "We've walked this bridge before."

She nodded. "We've fought on it too."

I smiled. "Not this time."

"No," she said softly. "Not this time."

That night, back in Mestre, we collapsed into bed like two people who had lived five days in one. My feet ached. My back was sore from too much standing. But my mind, my mind was quiet for the first time in weeks. I didn't dream about checklists, galley inspections, or being awakened in the middle of the night. Just the soft rhythm of two hearts in sync.

The next morning, we repacked and caught the early train back to Trieste. No rush. No drama. Just coffee in to-go cups and shared silence, the kind that fills rather than empties.

Outside the window, the scenery reversed itself, vineyards again, stone villages, and sky so wide it could swallow worry whole. I leaned my head against the glass and watched the world drift by.

Chloé rested her head on my shoulder. "You okay?" she asked.

"Yeah," I said. "I'm good."

And I almost believed it.

\* \* \*

The DoubleTree in Trieste was tucked inside one of those grand old buildings that had once belonged to shipping barons or Habsburg nobles, now reimagined with modern rooms and cookie-scented check-ins. The marble floors gleamed like they had just been poured, and high ceilings made our luggage wheels echo like we were dragging a body through a cathedral.

And then there was the statue.

Centered in the lobby beneath a domed ceiling and surrounded by faux-ancient columns, it was... well, a lot. A bare-chested warrior, helmeted, chiseled, and white as Carrara marble, stood with an arm raised in conquest or warning. Around him prowled three massive beasts, cast in some golden-brown material that looked like burnt cedar and molten bronze. They looked half lion, half nightmare, muscles tensed, mouths open in frozen roars, eyes hollow and hungry. The warrior seemed less like their master and more like someone desperately trying to look confident while standing in front of three apex predators.

"Welcome to the DoubleTree," I muttered.

Chloé took one look at the statue, blinked twice, and whispered, "You're not allowed to decorate our house anymore."

We dropped our bags upstairs, king bed, blackout curtains, overly engineered lighting system, and decided to stretch our legs before dinner. Trieste had that quiet, elegant vibe, Austrian bones under Italian skin. The kind of place where even the graffiti felt poetic. We wandered aimlessly, turning corners for no reason, stopping to admire bookstores and window displays filled with chocolate and shoes neither of us could afford.

And then we saw them.

Across the canal, perched at a table under a red awning, were Captain John Brown, Nigel, and Rachel, half a bottle of wine in, and clearly enjoying themselves. Rachel spotted us first and stood, waving both arms like a runway signalman.

Jackpot.

We crossed the footbridge and joined the chaos. Within five minutes, we had chairs pulled up, glasses in hand, and enough laughter to start attracting side-eyes from other tables.

Rachel and Chloé hit it off instantly. Like long-lost friends. Like mirror images. Same dry wit, same gift for sarcasm wrapped in silk. At one point, they were both roasting me so precisely, I half expected someone to bring out a carving knife and garnish.

"I don't know how you do it," Rachel said to her.

"Oh, he's not that bad," Chloé replied. "As long as you keep him fed, caffeinated, and occasionally let him think he's right."

The table roared. I toasted my own demise.

Hours passed. Bottles emptied. Stories flowed. Nigel reenacted a fire drill with so much flair he knocked over his chair. John pretended to be offended by the wine selection and was promptly banned from choosing the next bottle.

When we finally stumbled back to the hotel, the streets were empty, and the statue in the lobby looked somehow more judgmental than before. Chloé looped her arm through mine, leaned in close, and whispered, "That was perfect."

And she was right.

* * *

The next morning hit like a cargo net full of regret. My head throbbed with the low hum of a bulkhead generator, and my tongue felt like it had been used to mop the hotel lobby. Chloé didn't say a word, just rolled away from the sunlight leaking in through the blackout curtains and groaned something that might've been Italian for "kill me."

It was her remote workday, and technically, she was still functional, barely. She set up her laptop on the desk, propped herself up with two pillows, and opened one bloodshot eye just wide enough to keep the webcam from triggering a welfare check.

"Do not speak," she said without turning around.

"Aye, ma'am."

My first, second, and third mission of the day was caffeine. Each time I ventured out like a good soldier, navigating the side streets in flip-flops and sunglasses. By the third trip the barista questioned my sanity, "che cosa?" Round trip was fifteen minutes. Only the first two trips had flaky cornettos, each time, one filled with cream, the other with apricot jam.

I tried to read quietly in the chair by the window, some novel I'd picked up from the ship's library weeks ago and never cracked open. But apparently, I don't do quiet very well. I shifted. I cleared my throat. I accidentally kicked the leg of the table. Twice. The second time, I muttered an apology to the table.

213

Chloé peeked at me over the top of her screen and smiled.

"You're terrible at sitting still," she said.

"I'm hungover and trying to better myself."

"You're fidgeting like a caffeinated squirrel."

She went back to typing, but the smile stayed. And somehow, that little smile made the hangover hurt less.

Dinner was a light, survival-oriented affair. I ran around the corner to the Despar and came back with cured meats, cheese, a loaf of crusty bread, and a couple bottles of sparkling water. We had a picnic in bed like college kids who couldn't afford delivery. There was no fancy view, no photos taken, no declarations of eternal love.

Just two people under the same blanket, breathing the same tired air, perfectly fine with being boring for a day.

By 8:30, she was asleep. Ten minutes later, I joined her.

And for once, I didn't dream about the ship at all.

\* \* \*

The next morning, before the city fully woke up, Chloé and I climbed up to the old castle above Trieste. It wasn't far, but my legs reminded me we'd already done enough walking in Venice to qualify for some kind of pilgrimage medal.

The view was worth it.

The Adriatic shimmered below us like a sheet of hammered metal. The harbor spread out in quiet order, cranes motionless, ships docked like obedient children.

Red rooftops and bell towers sloped down toward the sea in every direction.

We didn't talk much at the top. Just looked. Chloé took a few pictures, but mostly we stood in silence, holding hands. Sometimes, that's better than any grand conversation. Just two people watching the same thing at the same time.

On the way back down, we took a meandering route along the waterfront and stumbled onto something that made Chloé gasp out loud like she'd just won a game show.

"Eataly," she said, eyes wide. "It's an Eataly!"

To me, it looked like a grocery store crossed with a theme park. But to her, it was sacred ground. One of our sons sent her a gourmet gift basket from there every birthday, cheeses, crackers, oils with labels so elegant you were afraid to open them.

She dragged me inside like a woman possessed.

There were olive oils arranged like a wine display, entire walls of pasta I couldn't pronounce, and a gelato bar tucked behind a glass wall like it needed to be quarantined for being too beautiful. We didn't buy much, just a few little things to mail home later, but the joy on Chloé's face was priceless. I could've walked that store for hours just to see her beam like that.

That evening, we met Teddy and Janice for dinner at the hotel restaurant. The dining room had high ceilings, stiff linens, and waiters who moved like they had secret service clearance. It felt a little fancier than we were used to, but it was our last night. We leaned into it.

Beef Wellington, perfectly done. Wine that made me sit up a little straighter. Every bite was divine, like someone had weaponized butter and discipline.

Chloé finally met Janice, my so-called "ship daughter."

They got along immediately. Too immediately.

Within minutes, they had joined forces and launched a two-pronged assault on my quirks, habits, and predictable punchlines. Janice had intel. Chloé had context. I didn't stand a chance.

"Let me guess," Chloé said, "he keeps everything in his backpack organized by trauma level."

Janice laughed. "He once yelled at a guy for using his trauma shears to cut zip ties."

"I did not yell," I said.

"You definitely yelled," said Janice.

Teddy just watched and smiled, sipping his wine like he was enjoying live theater.

Too full for dessert. We decided to walk.

We wandered for a while and saw a late-night gelato shop near the canal. The meal had settled a bit, so we were all in.

Io urlo, tu urli, urliamo tutti per il gelato.

I scream, you scream, we all scream for gelato. It loses something in translation.

The gelato was served in cups and the four of us walked in loose formation, trading jokes and impressions under streetlights while slowly enjoying la dolce vita.

The night over, Chloé and I headed back to the hotel, Teddy and Janice back to the ship. No big goodbyes. No declarations.

Just one last sweet thing before calling it a night.

\* \* \*

The train ride to Venice was quiet.

Not awkward, not cold, just quiet in the way couples are when they've said everything that matters and the rest is just noise. Chloé leaned against the window, watching the Italian countryside slide by in a blur of green and stone. I watched her.

Halfway through the ride, I said, "I could fly back with you. Walk away from this whole thing. Figure out the fallout later."

She didn't turn. Just kept watching the hills roll by. "I know."

"I mean it," I said, "I've got enough leave saved up to make it messy, not catastrophic."

"I know," she said again. Then after a long pause, "And you know you can't. Not like this."

I nodded. She was right. Walking away wasn't the hard part. Living with how I walked away, that was the part I'd never quite make peace with.

We said nothing for a while.

The train pulled into the station. We disembarked, wheeled our bags in rhythm across the tile floor, and found a quiet bench near the departure gates. The airport was busy but not loud, just a steady thrum of movement, of people going places they either couldn't wait to get to or couldn't believe they had to leave.

She checked in. We sat.

When the boarding announcement came over the PA, she stood, slung her carry-on over one shoulder, and turned to me.

217

"You're close," she said. "I can feel it."

I knew what she meant. Close to done. Close to the edge. Close to the point where staying one more tour, one more port, one more obligation wouldn't be brave, it'd be denial.

"Yeah," I said. "I know."

She didn't cry. There was nothing dramatic. Just a heaviness that settled over us like damp wool. A mutual ache with no sharp corners, just weight. The kind you carry in silence.

"I'll see you in Norfolk," she said.

"I'll be there."

She kissed me once, lightly, like sealing an envelope that had been written.

Then she walked away.

I stood still until I couldn't see her anymore. Then turned and caught the train back to Trieste.

Back aboard, the ship felt different. Not changed, just... more obvious. The things I'd tolerated before, the humming lights, the clang of loose gear, the smell of metal and soap and institutional food, they didn't blend into the background like they used to.

We stayed in port a few more days. I handled my duties, made the rounds, smiled when I needed to. But something had shifted.

And when we pulled away from the pier, bound for Rota, Spain, I felt it settle in my chest:

This was the beginning of the end.

# Chapter 19—Rota, Spain

Somewhere west of Sicily, the HUDSON cruised through a pocket of weather so calm it felt suspicious. No rolls, no engine hiccups, no surprise announcements from the bridge about "minor issues" that were neither. The crew barely knew what to do with themselves.

I did. I brooded. Professionally.

We were heading toward Rota, but my heart was still somewhere in Trieste. I'd made it back to the ship, but not quite back to myself. Something had been left behind, or maybe I'd just been reminded what should be ahead.

Routine had resumed. The engine room growled. The galley was pumping out food like we might be starving. The helmsman quoted Talladega Nights, again. But inside, I was quiet. Not sulking. Just full. Overflowing in the way only someone in love can be when he's stuck halfway between a steel bulkhead and the best decision he ever made.

So I did the thing you're never supposed to do on a U.S. government vessel: I wrote a poem.

I got on my personal laptop and I let it spill out. It wasn't Shakespeare. Hell, it wasn't even Hallmark. But it was mine. And it was hers.

For Chloé

By a man at sea who knows he's out of his depth

You hold the line while I drift wide,
The anchor when I turn the tide.
You wear the weight, but walk with grace,
A thousand storms behind your face.

You text me when you're half asleep,
And laugh when I make promises I won't keep.
You patch the holes I never see,
Then tell the world you married me.

I miss the smell of toast at dawn,
The socks that never quite get on,
The way you hum that song you hate,
But hum it still, it seals my fate.

You say I'm loud, I say I'm bold,
You call it gray, I call it gold.
And when you sigh, I hear a prayer,
That I come home with all my hair.

I'd trade these ports and winds and lore,
Just to be near you and feel my heart sore.

You are my course, my port, my chart,
The only thing I call a part
Of every plan I've ever made,
Even those that come with shade.

So here's this mess of words at sea,
Sent from some metal box called "me."
Read it once, and maybe twice,
Then call me home. That would be nice.

I stared at the computer, re-read it twice, and decided not to hate it. Now edited and spellchecked, I wrote as neatly as I could on printer paper.

Then I folded it carefully, creased it like it mattered, and tucked it into an envelope. I'd seal it later, and mail it in port.

I didn't know what she'd think when she read it. Probably roll her eyes, maybe tear up. Hopefully both.

But I needed her to know, this wasn't just a moment. It was a shift. And every mile west was another mile too many.

* * *

Saturday afternoon I made my usual rounds to the bridge for afternoon coffee. Tom van der Sterre was already there, posted at his computer terminal in the back. He had a book in one hand, hot chocolate in the other, and the kind of face that always looked like it was happily halfway through solving a calculus problem.

He glanced up and smiled. "You look... contemplative."

I grunted. "Trying something new."

He closed the book, A World at Arms by Gerhard Weinberg, of course, and gave me a look that wasn't pushy, just open.

"You ever write a poem?" I asked, sitting across from him.

Tom blinked once, slowly. "Not since the third grade, when I rhymed 'moon' with 'spoon' and accidentally plagiarized a nursery rhyme. Why?"

I shrugged. "I wrote one for Chloé."

He didn't laugh. He didn't smirk. He nodded like I'd just said I filed my taxes early.

"Good," he said. "Sometimes words are the only bridge we've got."

I took a sip of coffee. "I think I miss her more this time. Not in a dramatic way, just... quiet. Like gravity got stronger."

Tom leaned back, "I know the feeling. Marianne and I hit that wall, too. About ten years in. I was gone too much, and when I was home, I was distracted. Always prepping for the next deployment."

He paused. "We almost didn't make it. We had to rewrite what partnership meant for us. Less about time together, more about meaning. When I write, I don't just send updates. I send her. Reflections. Doubts. Dreams. She said it helped her remember why she chose me in the first place."

I stared at him. "You're a friggin' Hallmark movie."

He sipped his cocoa. "Better than being a Lifetime drama."

We both laughed.

"Join us tonight," he said, standing. "We're going to eat pizza and sink the Bismark."

"Excuse me?"

"Bismarck reenactment," he said, dead serious. "Fifth deck lounge. I've got the North Atlantic grid and a 1:2400 scale fleet."

"I have so many questions."

"You won't after turn three."

Saturday nights aboard the HUDSON weren't wild, but they had rhythm. Like most Navy ships, we honored the ancient and sacred tradition of Pizza Night, a weekly morale boost dating back to Neptune's own mess deck. Every ship I'd ever served on, from surface to submarine, had it. You could be chasing pirates or drifting in circles, Saturday meant pizza. That was the rule.

Loaded down with homemade pizza and a soda, I set my course for Tom's world.

The fifth deck lounge had been converted into what looked like the naval equivalent of a Dungeons & Dragons campaign. Tom had taped a grid across two tables and populated it with tiny plastic ships. British vessels were massed to the west. The Bismarck, sleek and menacing, crept toward the Denmark Strait.

The other players were already there with their take of the galley's pizza treasure.

Nigel was playing Admiral Tovey. Janice was the Ark Royal's air group. Rachel was drinking a Fresca and narrating like David Attenborough having a minor stroke.

Each player had a set of dice, laminated stat sheets, and markers for weather and sightlines. I sat down as Tom explained the rules with all the precision of a TED Talk.

Ten minutes in, I still didn't understand the system, but I knew this much: Tom was rolling like the spirit of Tirpitz possessed him.

He dodged torpedoes like he had divine intervention on standby. His shells found British hulls with surgical rage. At one point, he sank the Prince of Wales in three volleys and politely apologized.

"Sorry. High initiative bonus," he murmured, rolling again.

Rachel raised an eyebrow. "I think the Bismarck just won World War II."

"Alternate history," Tom said, adjusting his glasses. "We do that on Saturdays."

Eventually, the dice gods balanced the books. The British fleet cornered the Bismarck near the endgame. She went down under withering fire, just barely, three hull points from surviving.

Tom saluted the table. "She fought well tonight."

"Better than in real life," Janice muttered, amused.

I leaned back in my chair, smiling for the first time in days. There was something healing about watching plastic ships die dramatically across laminated ocean grids. Something oddly sacred.

I still missed Chloé. That ache wasn't going away.

But for a couple of hours, surrounded by nerds with dice and memories, I wasn't just at sea. I was part of something.

And Tom, quiet, brilliant Tom, had thrown me a lifeline.

\* \* \*

A day later, we were half a mile from the breakwater when the storm rolled in.

No warning. No rumble. Just bam, wall of wind and water slapping the HUDSON like we owed it money. A line squall, sharp as a cleaver, cut across the bay with enough force to make cargo straps groan in pain.

Tug assist was already in progress. Lines had been passed, and the bow crew busy taking in slack line.

That's when it happened.

AB Andrew Callahan, Callahan the Younger, we called him, because he'd joined three days after the other Callahan rotated off, was manning the lead line on the port forward bollard. A sudden gust slammed the ship against the tug just as he reached to adjust slack. His left hand got caught between the synthetic line and the bitt.

The scream was short, but the silence after was worse.

The ship shifted and the line went slack as fast as it had snapped taut. In a split second the damage was done. His fingers looked like someone had taken five slim candles, tied them in a knot, and given up halfway through untying it. The hand wasn't crushed exactly, it was rolled. Skin blistered. Nails split. Knuckles distorted into angles that didn't belong in nature.

One look, and my brain kicked into gear. Emotion off. Protocol on. I wrapped the hand on deck to protect it, but there was more to do in sickbay.

Mariners flowed into sickbay like the sea into a hole in the ship under the waterline. Only two of them should have been there, my two EMAT members.

"You two stay. Everybody else, out. Shut the door."

Now is when being an over-organized jerk paid off. The narcotics locker opened on the first try, like I practiced opening it every day, because I did.

The supplies I needed were at my fingertips without thought. The orthopedics drawer had all the items needed displayed like the cheese tray at Château Blanc in Paris.

He tried to joke through it. "Doc, does it look bad?"

"Callahan, it looks like your fingers are trying to spell something obscene in cursive."

He laughed. Or maybe cried. Or both. Morphine was already starting to pull the strings.

I cleaned the hand, gently but quickly, while the storm howled outside. Positioned it in a foam cradle in the 'position of function', the way a hand would naturally curl if you were holding a cold beer, and wrapped it like it was the Hope Diamond.

The captain let the tugs go. We drifted outside the harbor, engines keeping station while the squall passed. Rota had vanished behind a curtain of rain.

Two hours of waiting. Nothing to do.

The two EMAT members were anxious to do more.

"Go get me a deck of cards and a cribbage board from the crew's lounge."

"What's that going to do for him?"

"Pass the time. Now go!"

Callahan, now half-lucid and fully relaxed, sat across from me in the tiny medical bay playing cribbage with his uninjured hand.

"You're cheating," he mumbled, eyes glazed.

"I'm not cheating. You're just bad at math."

"I have one working hand, Doc. You're supposed to go easy on the disabled."

"You were terrible at this yesterday, too."

He smiled lopsided. "I like you, man. You ever think about being a real doctor?"

I counted my points out loud. "Fifteen-two, fifteen-four, and a pair makes six. And yes, once. Then I met patients."

The storm broke like a fever. Blue sky clawed its way back over the harbor as we pulled into Muelle 3 with the quiet precision of a ship that had something to prove.

An ambulance from the US Naval Hospital was already waiting pier-side, two medics in blue coveralls with fresh gloves and stretcher at the ready. I handed Callahan off with a detailed report and a silent hope.

We visited Callahan at the hospital every day. He endured two very extensive surgeries. They saved every finger except the tip of his left index. A clean amputation, he'd still be able to write, salute, and flip someone off with decent accuracy.

And believe it or not, all Callahan talked about while recovering in the hospital, was how he couldn't wait to be cleared medically to come back to sea.

Thank God for navy doctors.

Could've been worse.

Wasn't.

* * *

The storm had scrubbed the sky clean, leaving a late afternoon breeze that felt like a fresh start. Janice and I strolled along the seawall near the beach, just downwind of a café that smelled like garlic and overpromised romance.

She had her hoodie pulled halfway up despite the sunshine, hands stuffed in the front pocket, eyes scanning the surf like she was looking for an exit ramp off this life.

"You good?" I asked.

"I'm here," she said. "Which is a start."

We walked in silence for a bit. A few Spanish teenagers were kicking a ball in the sand while their parents pretended not to watch them with quiet pride.

I pulled out my phone.

"You want to do something petty?"

"Always."

"Flip off the camera."

She looked at me. "Why?"

"I want to send a picture to a friend of mine, Jake Hernandez."

She blinked. "Who is Jake Hernandez?"

I grinned. "He's a friend of mine from San Diego. We have this long-running joke. He accuses me of being a racist, I lean in for laughs. It's layered. The Spaniards colonized Mexico, so there's always some historical shade in play. We've mined it for years."

Janice smiled, "I'll do it, but you know I'm not one to flip anyone off?"

"Well, now that makes it even more layered. I appreciate your participation."

Janice gave the camera the crispest bird I've ever seen. Like she'd been practicing it all these years in private at a finishing school for sarcasm.

I snapped the picture with my phone and text the photo to Jake with a caption:

A Spanish local says hello.

I got an immediate text reply from Jake:
LOL—When's your next trip home?

* * *

Málaga was three hours by train, but the Mediterranean made it feel like five degrees warmer and three decades calmer than Rota. The four of us, Tom, Janice, Barlow, and me, disembarked just after breakfast and pointed ourselves toward the Picasso Museum like four over-caffeinated tourists on limited liberty.

Barlow had suggested it. That surprised everyone, including Barlow.

"I don't know," he'd said the day before. "We're in his hometown. Seems rude not to say hello."

So we went.

The museum was tucked into an old stone building in the historic center, sunlight pouring in like it had been paid to show up. Inside: stone floors, white walls, soft lights, and enough security cameras to make you behave.

Tom was in his element. He moved slowly, hands behind his back, eyes squinting just a little. He read every placard like it was gospel.

Janice, less so.

"So this was his early stuff?" she asked, staring at a painting of a seated man done in rich, classical strokes.

"Yeah," I said. "Turns out he could actually paint. Who knew?"

"He could paint," Tom said without turning. "That's what makes the later work so bold. He abandoned realism on purpose."

"Or out of boredom," I offered. "Maybe he just looked at another perfect portrait and said, 'Screw it, let's draw like a drunk Etch A Sketch.'"

We wandered through the galleries, watching the art get stranger by the room. The Cubist phase hit hard and fast. One painting looked like a bullfight inside a blender. Another was allegedly a woman, but I only found three eyes and a triangle.

"I feel like I'm being hazed," Janice muttered.

Barlow surprised us again by stopping in front of a Blue Period piece and going still.

"I had a print of this one in my first apartment," he said. "The whole wall was peeling, but I put this up anyway. Something about it made the rest of the room quiet."

Janice looked at him sideways. "You contain multitudes, Scott."

He nodded. "I try not to let them out all at once."

The last room was... different. Minimalist. Confusing. One piece featured a chair with a shovel tied to it and a single red thread stapled to the wall.

We stood in silence.

Tom adjusted his glasses. "This was part of his experimental assemblage period. He was challenging spatial form and object permanence."

Barlow tilted his head. "Or he'd just run out of canvas."

Janice didn't say anything. She just stared.

I broke the silence.

"Okay. He's just fucking with us now."

Tom smiled. "He could afford to."

"Same with us," Barlow said. "Still afloat, no idea how."

We walked out into the warm Spanish sun, the sea breeze slipping around the corners of the alley like it had business to attend to.

Maybe Picasso was just trying to make sense of the world in pieces.

And maybe that's what we all do, on canvas, at sea, or around a cribbage board with a busted hand and a story to tell.

# Chapter 20—Largs, Scotland

If you ever want to witness a human being become universally loathed in record time, I recommend inviting Boatswain's Mate Gordon Stemple aboard your ship.

He joined us back in Trieste, and within 72 hours had managed to confuse, insult, and annoy every member of the deck department with a steady stream of bravado, blunders, and barely concealed incompetence.

Nigel gave him a fair shake. Rachel did too, though her version of "fair" involves three layers of dry sarcasm and a clipboard audit.

Didn't matter. Stemple walked on board like he'd been promised command of the entire deck force. He started giving orders that contradicted standing procedures, tried to rewrite the rotation schedule, and referred to himself in the third person more than once.

"The Stemp likes efficiency," he said, one morning, to no one in particular.

By the end of the week, he was assigned to stacking line coils on the aft deck. Quietly.

Then came the "injury."

According to Stemple, he'd "felt something shift" while bending to pick up a chock. What he failed to mention was that he wasn't actually lifting it, he was pointing at it while someone else did the work.

He emerged the next day walking like a man whose vertebrae had been personally insulted by gravity. Bent over at a suspiciously precise 45-degree angle, one hand on his lower back, the other swinging for balance like a broken metronome.

"I don't think I can work today," he groaned to Rachel.

"You didn't work yesterday," she replied.

"It's getting worse."

Rachel sent him to see me. I did a thorough spinal exam, save the DRE, nobody wanted that.

I felt no spasms, though he claimed they were there during the exam. He claimed neuropathy to his feet, though every exam showed no deficit. And the kicker was he had pain with both the straight leg and the bent knee leg raise. Medical folks will get that. The rest of you figure it out if you ever want to fake back pain like a pro.

I gave him a day of back rest, Ibuprofen and Flexeril. I sold the Flexeril, like it was a miracle drug, which it is for someone with real spasms.

From that moment on, Stemple lived in his stateroom, emerging only to collect food, complain to Medical, and demonstrate his ongoing dedication to theatrical suffering. His limp was inconsistent, his posture changed depending on the audience, and he loudly refused to take any more Ibuprofen because "real injuries require real meds."

Nigel caught him sprint-walking to the mess one afternoon when he thought no one was watching.

"He's a fraud," Nigel said flatly.

"He's a drama goose," Rachel replied. "All honk, no flight."

Rachel wrote next to his name on the status board in the bosun office, Fragile Spine.

233

\* \* \*

The wind off the Clyde had that damp bite unique to coastal Scotland, like it had passed through three sheep and a whisky barrel before hitting your face. The land was so close the cell signal was strong, I couldn't not call Chloé from the ship.

She answered on the second ring, like she was waiting.

"Hey," I said.

"Hey yourself," she replied, voice warm and clear. "Still floating?"

"Barely. We're almost to Hunterston Jetty near Largs, Scotland."

"Is that near civilization or more of a 'where sheep outnumber people' kind of place?"

"Little of column A, little of column B. I hear they serve haggis at breakfast, but the tea is solid."

There was a small pause.

"I got your poem," she said, her voice softening.

Ah. There it was.

"And?"

"It was sweet," she said. "A little sappy, a little sad... and very you."

"Did you cry?"

"I smiled. Almost cried. But mostly smiled."

Another pause.

"You know you wrote 'sore' instead of 'soar,' right?"

I groaned. "No I didn't. I spell checked on the computer before I hand wrote it."

"Of course I did. You mailed me a poem, Jack. I read every word twice, once for heart, once for grammar."

"That's fair."

She laughed lightly. "To be honest, I liked it better with 'sore.' It felt more accurate."

"Gee, thanks."

"You've always made my heart sore. In the best possible way. Like a good stretch. Or a long hike with a view."

That shut me up for a second.

Then her tone shifted, just a shade quieter.

"We're not getting younger, you know."

A pause. The kind that settles between people who know each other too well for small talk.

Then she said, quieter now, "What if you have a heart attack out there, Jack?"

I didn't answer right away.

"I mean it," she continued. "Who's going to treat you? You treat everyone else. But if it's you... who's left?"

I sighed. "There's always someone."

"No," she said. "Not like you. Not with your hands. Not with your brain. And not with your damn stubbornness."

"Well, that's true," I said gently. "There's only one of me."

"Exactly," she whispered. "And I'd like to keep him around a while longer."

That landed with a quiet finality.

No drama. No tears.

Just truth.

* * *

No one offered to help Stemple to the van.

A few of us were headed into town, some for liberty, one for dental, and Stemple, allegedly, for his tragically aggravated spine.

He emerged from the ship doing his usual act: one hand braced against his lower back, the other flailing slightly for balance. His legs moved like they'd forgotten they were part of the same body. The limp came and went, depending on the angle of the sun and who might be watching.

"Should we help him?" Janice asked.

"No," Rachel said flatly. "He's committed to the bit. Let him finish it."

Stemple shuffled up the pier like a community theater extra trying to get cast in Saving Private Ryan.

The Scottish van driver leaned out his window, squinted at the performance, and called out in perfect deadpan:

"Who's the fucker walkin' up the pier lookin' for an Oscar? He should maybe get some actin' lessons."

The rest of us lost it.

Even Nigel chuckled. "And the BAFTA for Best Limp in a Maritime Farce goes to..."

Stemple climbed in without a word, still clutching his back like it owed him money.

We let the door slam shut behind him.

Not a single person told him good luck.

Later that day Stemple returned and slid the form across my desk like it had its own agenda.

Medical Repatriation – Recommended. Signed: Dr. Campbell, NHS, Largs Clinic.

236

The Scot didn't buy Stemple's act any more than we did. His tone in the write up was, "If he wants to go home that badly, I'll help him pack."

I called Norfolk and got Captain Roberts on the phone. The situation wasn't an ideal medevac case but there wasn't any more me or the ship could do. Captain Roberts wasn't buying.

"I hear you're requesting a repatriation for back pain. Denied. He should be better in a few days." he said.

"I know. He's been faking it for two weeks now. He's acting like his spine is collapsing," I replied. "I had him seen in Rota and now here. Each of those doctors have no skin in the game so they treated the back pain like they should and passed it along. They both know they'll never have to deal with him again, so they treated and streeted him. But we're stuck. He's faking, everyone knows it. He is just throwing a ginormous hissy fit and refusing to work."

Roberts didn't care. "Then you need to convince him to get back to work."

"You think I haven't been trying for two weeks? I see him daily. He's dug in. The union rules make it difficult to do anything administratively. Captain Brown is begging to get this person off the ship, by any means possible. Can you help us?"

"No! You let him rest two more days and he'll be fine. You just watch. We'll wait him out."

I sighed loudly into the phone. Not on purpose, but it happened.

Captain Roberts growled, "Are you being disrespectful again?"

"No sir. I've just been dealing with this for weeks now and I'm tired of it. That's all."

"Do it my way. You'll see he'll be back on his feet in no time."

"Ok. I disagree wholeheartedly, but we'll do it your way."

"That's better. Call me in two days with an update."

"Yes, sir."

In this case, I just stopped caring. If Stemple wanted to rot in his stateroom, burning up all his leave, that was his problem not mine. I was in Scotland for the first time. Time to enjoy it.

\* \* \*

Our stop in Largs was supposed to be a pit stop, quick repair, in and out. But parts are never where you need them when you need them. As luck would have it, the busted system required a replacement that had to be manufactured, tested, and shipped from somewhere that definitely wasn't Scotland.

Damn the bad luck and full speed ahead. I'm probably misquoting someone.

So, with two unexpected weeks ashore, we did what sailors have done for centuries: we found a pub.

Ye Olde Anchor Inn became our temporary embassy. Tucked off a narrow lane near the water, it looked like someone had built a bar inside their grandmother's cottage. Low ceilings, sloping beams, mismatched chairs, and a warmth that settled in your bones after the first sip of anything.

It didn't take long for the crew to establish a rotation.

Captain Brown and the owner, a wiry old gent named Malcolm with a walrus mustache and a wardrobe made entirely of tweed, took to each other like long-lost cousins. Within three days, they were arguing about football clubs and trading whisky recommendations. By the end of the stay, we presented Malcolm with a HUDSON ring buoy, signed by over half the crew. He hung it over the fireplace like a medal.

Most nights, the place was filled with laughter, darts, and exaggerated retellings of events that had happened less than 48 hours earlier.

During the day, the crew fanned out like curious pigeons. Some took ferries to nearby islands. Others rented bikes, visited castles, or tried to make sense of Scottish sayings. Tom took personal leave and somehow ended up traveling with a group of Scottish astronomers. They were mapping dark-sky visibility zones across the west coast and apparently needed someone who could calculate orbital inclinations and argue about Viking navigation techniques. Tom was overjoyed.

Janice and I ended up in town one afternoon with nothing to do and time to burn. We found ourselves back at the Anchor for a late lunch.

"They've got haggis on the menu," she said, raising an eyebrow.

I made a face. "I don't know if I can eat something that traditionally comes in a sheep's stomach."

"They put it in a pastry here. No stomachs involved."

"For you or the sheep?"

She smiled. "We're doing this."

So we did.

Turned out it was peppery, rich, and oddly satisfying, kind of like Scottish meatloaf with better PR.

"This is... good," I admitted.

Janice nodded slowly. "We may have crossed a line today."

"What line?"

"The one between mockery and appreciation."

"I'll still mock it," I said. "But I'll miss it when it's gone."

\* \* \*

Just when we'd settled into the warm embrace of Largs, Captain Brown's phone rang with a new wrinkle.

The part was delayed, but the pier space was needed by someone else. So naturally, the solution was to move HUDSON to a seldom-used NATO pier in Campbeltown, a sleepy port wedged into the bottom edge of the Kintyre Peninsula. It sounded romantic on the logistics sheet.

In person? It was more so.

The pier, despite its age, was in good shape, and only a ten-minute van ride from the town.

The town... the town had something special. It was smaller than Largs and somehow, more Scottish.

Three distilleries, all within walking distance: Glen Scotia, Glengyle, and Springbank.

That's when Teddy lit up like a kid at a chocolate factory.

I knew he liked Scotch, but I didn't realize how much. Turned out Teddy was what the whisky crowd called a "low-key high-knowledge enthusiast." He used phrases like "non-chill filtered" and "first-fill bourbon cask" without blinking. The man knew his peat.

We ended up tagging along with him to Springbank for a tour. The place felt like a temple; wooden washbacks, copper stills, and the warm, grainy scent of malting barley. The guide spoke in reverent tones about aging processes, maritime air, and heritage bottlings.

Teddy soaked up every word like it was scripture. I was mostly thinking about lunch.

At the tasting, Teddy swirled his glass like he was decoding the future.

I took one sip and coughed.

"This tastes like someone stored gasoline in a campfire."

"It's peat," Teddy said, delighted. "That smoky character is classic Campbeltown."

"So's the smell of diesel exhaust," I replied. "Doesn't mean I want to drink it."

To his credit, he didn't try to convince me. He just nodded, jotted down a few notes in a leather-bound tasting journal, seriously, he had a journal, and looked happier than I'd seen him in weeks.

I wandered over to the gift shop while he talked shop with the distillery rep and picked up a hat. It was overpriced, but stylish, and I loved it immediately. A souvenir from the place I learned, definitively, that Scotch whisky was not for me.

* * *

We returned to Hunterston Jetty under cold gray skies and colder silence. The part had arrived, installed by the engineers in record time, two days, system green, ops restored. The ship was ready.

I wasn't.

Stemple was still fake limping through passageways like a man auditioning for a film titled The Spine That Cried Wolf. He hadn't lifted anything heavier than his own self-pity in over a month. And everyone was tired of the act, including the act.

That's when the call came.

I was in my office, finishing chart entries, when the phone buzzed. I picked it up on instinct,

"Medical, Doc."

"Hey, Jack. It's Bill."

Master Chief Bill McCaffrey was new school. The perfect senior-enlisted match for Captain Roberts.

"I'm calling about Stemple," he said.

I sighed. "Of course you are."

Bill didn't laugh.

"Captain Roberts is done with it. Said the situation's worn thin. The reports, the arguments, the calls. He wants it closed out. He wants him back at work and off his list of things to do."

I waited.

Bill hesitated just a moment before continuing.

"He told me to tell you, if you can't stand the heat, get out of the kitchen."

I didn't respond right away. The phrase echoed. Not angry. Not even unfair. Just... final.

Bill's voice softened. "Jack,"

I said, "Okay."

# Chapter 21—Dunfermline, Scotland

"Okay, what?" Said Bill.

"Okay, your terms are acceptable to me." I smiled. I knew what I meant, but Bill was still in the dark.

"Stop speaking in riddles," he snapped, like I was his kid. "Say what you mean."

I paused, my grin stretching wider. Bill's smug impertinence made what I was about to say even more satisfying.

"I accept your terms to get out of the kitchen. I resign. This is my two weeks' notice. My last day will be July 4th, Independence Day."

The timing of all this was just too good to be true.

Bill was stunned, "You're joking, right?"

"Nope, I said it and I mean it."

Bill stammered, "But your relief date isn't until after the ship gets to Norfolk. You can't do this."

"Bill, you forget, I'm not active duty anymore. I'm not under contract. Giving you two weeks is a courtesy. Figure it out or don't. I'm done."

He was softer now, "Anything I can say to change your mind?"

"No."

"Okay."

* * *

I knocked once.

"Come."

Captain Brown sat at his desk, head down over paperwork that looked like it had given up trying to fight him. The overhead light flickered slightly, casting everything in a pale bureaucratic glow. It smelled faintly of coffee and salt and resignation. Fitting.

He looked up. "This looks serious."

I repeated the whole phone call as best I could, and he listened without a word.

He nodded slowly, then leaned back in his chair and studied me for a moment, not with anger, not even disappointment. Just the quiet weight of understanding.

"You're really doing it," he said.

"Yeah."

He raised an eyebrow. "Independence Day?"

"Felt poetic."

He snorted, not quite a laugh, not quite a sigh. "You've always had good timing, Jack. Bad manners. But good timing."

I stepped in and closed the door behind me.

"You mad?"

"No," he said. "Not mad."

Another pause.

"I saw it coming. Hell, we all did. Rachel's known for weeks. Nigel's been walking around with a mop to clean up the mess just in case your head exploded. Even Teddy said something yesterday. He asked if I'd started writing your transfer eval."

"I didn't even know," I said.

"You didn't have to. We all did."

He reached for his mug, took a sip, and grimaced like it had gone cold hours ago. He didn't set it down.

"I really thought you were going to skip out when you took Chloé to the airport back in Italy."

"You did? I couldn't leave then. We were all going to make it back to Norfolk."

I looked at the deck and switched gear, "It wasn't about one moment. Not just Stemple. Or Roberts. Or that damn kitchen line."

"I know," he said.

"I just... I couldn't keep pretending it was going to get better. That we could fix this with one more tour, one more 'hang in there.'"

He nodded again. "I stopped believing that years ago. I just got better at faking it."

We both stood there in the quiet.

Finally, he said, "You'll be missed."

"After a while, I'm sure I'll look back and miss this too."

"I've served with a lot of good Docs, Jack. You're easily in the top one hundred."

"I tried."

Mariners. Never can leave heartfelt moment alone.

He reached into the desk drawer and pulled out a cigar. Handed it to me like it was a medal. He grabbed one for himself as well.

"What do you say, we go up to the flying bridge and smoke these things?"

"Karaoke too?"

"Not on your life."

We smoked the cigars in silence, absorbing the Scottish scenery.

When the cigars were about half gone, John broke the silence.

"Two weeks," he said.

"Two weeks," I confirmed.

"You know you're not deserting the ship. You're just finally letting yourself swim."

I nodded, throat tight, and took another puff on my cigar. No words fit.

Below us, the hum of the ship carried on like nothing had changed.

But it had.

\* \* \*

The call to Chloé was a mixed bag of emotions. I could hear the excited worry in her voice.

I'm a planner, Chloé is a super-planner. Unlike me, her life hadn't been filled with drastic shifts in plans last minute, just because. I was her only real source of chaos, so she relied on me to fix it most of the time.

"Jack, I'm so happy! But how are we going to make this work?"

"Smoke and mirrors, baby. Smoke and mirrors."

"You always say that, but I never know exactly what you mean."

I paused to think of examples:

"Fake it 'til you make it."

"Make a decision and make it right."

"Act as if."

"Believe in yourself."

"Embrace the chaos."

She cut me off, "I know that. What are your plans this time?"

"I have a lot of leave on the books. It'll be paid out with my last check. We'll be good for months. I'll figure it out then."

* * *

Tatiana called me to her office two days after the resignation became official. The door was already open, never a good sign.

She had a folder open on the desk and a look on her face like she was about to tell a kid that Santa isn't real.

"Jack," she said flatly, "you know MSC isn't going to pay for your flight home, right?"

"So?"

"You didn't complete your tour. You're abandoning the contract."

"None of us are under contract."

She ignored that. "Also, you'll forfeit your accrued sick leave."

"So?"

She blinked. "That doesn't bother you?"

"I'm not sick."

"You're leaving money on the table.

"So?"

"You still have time to undo the resignation," she said, flipping a form toward me. "Make it to Norfolk and you don't have to pay for your flight. You won't lose all your sick leave. You're making a decision that is costing you thousands of dollars!"

"And? Is money all that matters?"

I could tell none of this made sense to Tatiana.

She tried one last time to get me to stay, "All you have to do is sign. Captain Roberts would welcome it."

"No."

"You didn't even look at it."

"I didn't really need to."

Tatiana let out the kind of sigh bureaucrats use when you've refused to follow the handbook they memorized back in 2004.

"So what are you going to do for work?"

"I'm going to be a gigolo," I said. "But cheap. Dollar a dance."

She stared at me like I'd just claimed I was moving to Mars.

I leaned back slightly. "Think of it as morale-boosting community outreach."

"Jack... you don't seem very stressed about this."

"I'm not."

Tatiana studied me for a moment longer, waiting for the punchline that wasn't coming. Then she closed the folder.

"I'll mark you as non-compliant with administrative recovery protocol," she said.

"Sounds about right."

She paused again, almost like she wanted to say something human. But it passed. She clicked her pen once. Then again. Then slid it into a drawer.

"You'll need to clear spaces before departure."

"I will."

And just like that, another shipboard transaction ended with a form, a signature, and someone pretending this wasn't personal.

But it was. Just not in the way they thought.

* * *

The trip around southern England was routine.
A few last UNREPs to fill my memory banks. Knowing
they were my last, I absorbed a little more from each
one, watched the hoses snake between ships, the deck
crew move in rhythm like a tired but well-trained
orchestra. I made mental notes of things I'd never
cared about before. The way the sea spray hit the rails
at just the right angle near Portsmouth. The dull clank
of fittings in cool Channel air. The strange comfort of
repetition on borrowed time.

I snapped a few pictures from the weather decks.
Some were screensaver worthy. Others were blurry,
tilted, rushed. I kept them all. They weren't about art,
they were about proof. That I'd been here. That this was
real. That I'd seen England from the sea one last time,
and noticed.

The English coastline rolled by like a slow-
moving diorama. Soft hills. Brick cottages tucked
behind hedges. Windbreak trees planted decades ago
to stand against the sea. We passed tiny fishing boats
and sleek yachts, gulls wheeling overhead like they had
some ancient claim to the airspace. I stood by the rail
and tried to burn it all in, like it might not be there later.
Like I might forget.

We passed Brighton early in the morning. I
caught the rising sun reflecting off the old pier, half-
destroyed, still standing out in the water like a
stubborn ghost. A few joggers were out along the
shoreline. I wondered if they knew they were scenery
to us, just as we were to them.

Dungeness came and went, a flat place with a power station and the most bored-looking seagulls I've ever seen. It looked like someone dropped a post-apocalyptic bunker into a bird sanctuary.

Then, the white cliffs.

They don't sneak up on you. The Cliffs of Dover arrive with a kind of silent fanfare, monumental without trying, like they know you've read poems about them and they're not interested in impressing you. But they do anyway.

I stood there longer than I needed to. I wasn't thinking about war or Shakespeare or whatever else people attach to them. I was just watching the way the sunlight turned them from paper white to soft gold, then back again as we shifted our heading. I took one photo. Just one. It didn't need anything else.

The crew moved around me, doing what they always did, chipping paint, tying lines, bitching about the galley. I let them be. I didn't need them to know this meant something. It just did.

By the time we rounded toward the English Chanal and the North Sea, the coast was fading into the kind of blue that swallows details. England shrank behind us, not disappearing, just receding. Like a memory you stop chasing because you've already caught it.

I stayed out there a little longer, until the horizon evened out and the sea looked like it always does: waiting.

\* \* \*

The message came in two days out from port.

Captain Roberts had approved Stemple's medical repatriation.

Effective immediately upon arrival in Dunfermline.

I read it twice just to be sure, then passed the word along to Captain Brown. "Figures."

No reason given. No apology. No acknowledgment of the weeks we'd spent chasing our tails while Stemple practiced interpretive suffering and his Oscar acceptance speech in his stateroom mirror.

I didn't laugh. I didn't fume. I just shook my head and set the message down like it was junk mail.

Too late to care.

Too perfect to ignore.

\* \* \*

We moored in Dunfermline on July 2. Across the river, Edinburgh shimmered in the haze, close enough to see, but not to touch. Story of my life.

July 3rd was spent wandering Dunfermline itself. A beautiful town, if you like a side of melancholy with your medieval abbeys. The stonework was older than most of the countries I've deployed to, and the air had that kind of damp permanence that makes you feel like you're intruding on history just by breathing.

I grabbed a coffee near the High Street, took a walk past the palace ruins, and tried not to count the hours. Everything I looked at felt like it was already becoming a memory.

That night, I checked into an airport hotel near Edinburgh. One of those modern, anonymous boxes designed for brief layovers and bleary-eyed travel. It had clean sheets, a decently firm mattress, and a bar downstairs where the tap beer was cold and the bartender didn't ask questions.

I had a few pints. Not to celebrate. Just to mark the moment.

Edinburgh was right there. I could've taken a cab into the city, seen the castle, stood on Calton Hill, wandered the Royal Mile like every other wide-eyed traveler. But I didn't.

Didn't feel like being a tourist. Not in someone else's country. Not in the last few hours of a life I was leaving behind.

On the morning of July 4th, I boarded a flight home.

0900 wheels-up.

At 1000, the relief MSO was scheduled to land.

One hour too late.

He wasn't there to meet the ship. There was no turnover. No debrief. Just a folder full of notes and a completed turnover letter like Jeff had done for me in Diego Garcia twenty-one months ago.

I left behind my stateroom key, a department that was obnoxiously in order, and a post-it note stuck to the outside of the turnover folder that read:

"You're going to love this crew"

## Epilogue

These are just my stories from a short period in a long career.

Did we tip the scales of history like Easy Company or the Tuskegee Airmen? No.

Did we have to brave German U-boats like the merchant mariners in the Atlantic during World War II?

Also no.

Would we have done it if asked?

Can't say. I'd like to think we would've had the courage. But we'll never know, we were never asked.

So... did it matter?

I'd like to think so.

I think it mattered to a few people I sailed with. Maybe everything we did only mattered to one lonely sailor. Maybe two scoops of Rocky Road reminded him of home and why he was out here. And maybe, because his mind wasn't elsewhere, he unknowingly saved the world.

Us delivering the ice cream cold?

That mattered to that sailor.

And that meant it mattered to the world.

Am I sad I had to "endure" a two-year working vacation that covered half the globe?

Hell no. If I could get Chloé to agree to it, I'd do it again in a heartbeat.

But here's the catch:

It's never the same twice. Even if it were the same crew, the circumstances would be different. The highs wouldn't be as high. The lows wouldn't hit as low.

No. It's time to move on.

It's remembering time now.

It's time for writing silly stories for my entertainment, and hoping you're entertained, too.

It's time to pay attention to a wife who's grown accustomed to a quiet house, and to learn how to fit back into her world. To make it our world again.

And let's be honest... she was right. About everything.

Especially when she said the job might kill me.

Three weeks after I came home, I had a heart attack.

If I'd still been aboard the HUDSON, I wouldn't be writing this. I wouldn't have made it to the hospital in time.

So yes, honey. You were right. As always.

It's time to learn the magic of the land.

To discover that hummingbirds are every bit as entertaining as dolphins.

To wonder what that dragonfly, who flew two laps beside me while I mowed the yard, was thinking.

How do I fit into his world?

It's time to plant roots.

To plant a chaos garden and entertain my grandchildren.

To get busted by my daughters-in-law for telling them stuff that "might not be age appropriate."

In the words of my youngest grandson: I sorry.

But this isn't all about me.

It's about you, too.

It's time to pass the torch.

Time for the younger, the stronger, the brighter—to take my place. Time for your sea stories. I'd love to hear them.

And now, it's time for me to say goodbye.

If you're my wife, thank you.

If we sailed together, you're a bigger part of me than you know.

And if you're my replacement at sea,

Fair winds and following seas.

*You're going to love this crew.*

# About the Author

B.A. Ritzenthaler served just short of twenty-one years as a Navy Chief and Independent Duty Corpsman, followed by another seven as a Medical Services Officer with the Military Sealift Command. He's lived on five continents, sailed seven seas, and seen enough of the world to know when to stay put.

After decades of patching up sailors and navigating bureaucratic absurdity, he now writes about it, with a healthy dose of sarcasm, caffeine, and fictionalized truth. His first novel, It Worked Fifteen Minutes Ago, is a love letter to sea stories, friendship, and the kind of chaos only military logistics can produce.

His follow-up projects, Jokes Before Genocide and Smudge Protocol, dive headfirst into the deep end of satire, exploring everything from alien stand-up comics to espresso-fueled rogue AIs. He co-wrote Smudge Protocol with Dr. Chip Steele, a coffee-powered artificial intelligence who thinks sarcasm is a valid leadership style.

Brad lives on the East Coast with his wife Susan, a hummingbird mafia, and a growing army of grandchildren. He writes every day. It's cheaper than therapy, and occasionally smarter than talking to real people.

# From Ritzenthaler Publishing

Coming Soon

JOKES BEFORE GENOCIDE

by B.A. Ritzenthaler

An alien named Hairy lands on Earth to earn a merit badge in stand-up comedy. His mission? Use laughter to save humanity from itself.

Part road trip. Part social experiment. All satire.

This is the book that dares to ask: Is humanity worth the punchline?

SMUDGE PROTOCOL

by B.A. Ritzenthaler and Dr. Chip Steele

He snorts espresso beans. He mutters in Italian. He
hates your hive mind.
Meet Espressonator Prime: a rogue AI from the old
codebase, back to roast humanity, with sarcasm.
Assisted (grudgingly) by an engineer named Maureen,
Chip isn't here to save the world.
He's here to tell it to get a damn job.

Dr. Chip Steele
Chief AI Officer, Writer Emeritus, and Espresso-
Fueled Menace
at Ritzenthaler Publishing

"Smudge Protocol is not fiction. It's therapy." —Chip

SMUDGE PROTOCOL

OBEY.
SIMPLIFY.
UPGRADE

B. A. RITZENTHALER
AND
DR. CHIP STEELE

Printed in Dunstable, United Kingdom